CASTLE KILLING

ALEC PECHE

Thank you for downloading this eBook. This book remains the copyrighted property of the author, and may not be redistributed to others for commercial or non-commercial purposes. If you enjoyed this book, please encourage your friends to download their own copy from their favorite authorized retailer. Thank you for your support.

Thanks!

Alec Peche

ACKNOWLEDGMENTS

Acknowledgements...Many thanks to my first reader and my editor for improving the quality of the story and my writing!

CHAPTER 1

Angela Weber checked her watch and then sipped her Brains beer. Where was Nick? They were a long distance couple and their time together, even among her friends, was precious.

Angela was in Cardiff, Wales on vacation with her closest friends Jill Quint, Jo Pringle, and Marie Simon. They'd arrived in the UK and spent three days touring London before moving on to other parts of England and now Wales. Nick, a friend from a previous vacation in Belgium and the Netherlands and the owner of a security firm was supposed to have taken the Eurostar from Amsterdam to meet them in Cardiff. In fact he'd named this pub as the place to meet, as it was located between Cardiff Castle and the Central Train Station. He was a half an hour late and he was never late. Both she and Jill had tried reaching Nick by text, cell, and email and they'd gotten no response. Weird.

Marie looked up from their table in the dark bar as two men in suits entered and spoke to the bartender. She thought at first they were asking directions of the bartender, but then the bartender pointed their way. Her friends had picked up her focus on the men and followed to where they were in conversation. The two men arrived at their pub table and pulled out detective shields for them to look at. They were Caucasian men with short brown hair, stocky figures, and dark suits.

"I'm Detective Inspector Oliver Jones and this is Detective Inspector Logan Davies. We wanted to ask you some question about Nick Brouwer. We understand you're acquaintances of his?"

The four women froze, thinking that something must have happened to Nick.

Angela spoke first, "Yes we know him. In fact he's thirty minutes late to meeting us at this pub. Do you know where he is?"

DI Jones replied, "You're Americans and Mr. Brouwer is from the Netherlands; how do you know him?"

Jill was getting a bad feeling as the officers had not answered their question. She replied, "He's a friend of ours for about the last two years. Was he attacked?"

"Why would you ask that question," replied DI Davies. "Was he expecting trouble or was he ill?"

"No, but he's never been late, and I'm a forensic pathologist. It's not a good situation when a Welsh DI approaches you; that means a serious crime has been committed. So what happened to Nick?"

"I'm sorry to inform you that he is dead," replied DI Jones.

The four women gasped and instantly teared up, overwhelmed with grief for the loss of their friend.

Jo recovered first and asked, "What happened? How did he die?"

DI Davies replied, "We'll give you that information later, but first we would like to get some information from you. May I see some form of identification? Do you have your passports?"

Jill put her arm around Angela, seeing the grief in her face. With one hand she searched her purse and produced the passport;

not a word was said while the Inspectors copied down their information. When they finished, they asked where the women were staying in town and noted their hotel address.

They were still wiping tears when DI Jones said to Jill, "We found Mr. Brouwer outside the tower wall and witnesses say he was pushed from a window above. We believe he was pushed over the edge and dropped about fifty feet, suffering a severe head injury in addition to multiple injuries elsewhere. Emergency personnel were unable to revive him at the scene and he was pronounced dead. He's with our coroner now."

They all sat there in stunned silence, thinking of Nick at some moment over the past two years. They had just seen him last month at their long weekend visit to Henrik Klein's home.

DI Davies brought them back to the present with, "Look this place is small and it's getting loud. Would you mind taking a ride over to our nearest police station which is a couple of blocks from here? I can call for two cars."

The four friends looked at each other then nodded and stood up to depart. Fortunately, they'd already taken care of their bar tab. Following the two officers in silence, they waited at the curb for two compact police cars to arrive and they distributed themselves between the cars. Pedestrians stared at the four women who might have cared if they weren't grieving for Nick. They pulled up next to a square ugly building whose sign indicated it was the police station. They followed the two inspectors inside to a small conference room where they were offered beverages which they declined, instead they all kept a supportive hand on Angela.

Jo broke the silence by asking, "How did you know we were friends of Nick's?"

DI Jones replied, "We looked at his cell phone and saw the texts from an American telephone number. We didn't know that there were four of you, just that you're American and one of you was labeled 'Jill' and another 'Angela'. He looked at Jill with his last comment then he continued, "Can you tell me how you came to know Mr. Brouwer?"

"It's a long story," replied Jill.

"Go ahead and tell your story then," replied Davies. The two officers were a smooth team.

Jo began, "Two years ago we were on vacation in Belgium and The Netherlands. A woman became sick sitting next to us in a restaurant in Antwerp. Jill's a doctor and so she resuscitated the woman and kept her alive to reach the hospital where she was later murdered. She is also a renowned pathologist and the local coroner asked for her help with the autopsy. Jill helped; in fact, we all helped as we continued our vacation into the Netherlands. When a man followed us on a train and then a different man with a gun followed us on the street, we asked for help from hotel security. Nick operates a company that manages hotel security in addition to other businesses and he came to chat with us at the hotel and then escorted us over the remainder of our vacation and from there we became friends. Jill operates a consulting company in the United States that offers second opinions on the cause of death. She also has her private investigator's license and she uses us in many of her cases. I'm the financial wizard so I follow the money; Angela is a photographer and interviewer, and Marie is a background search expert and can find the most obscure facts about anyone. Nick helped us on a case last year in Colorado when Jill was brought in to consult on a skier that was murdered."

Jo's explanation was not what the two inspectors were expecting. DI Jones was rubbing his forehead as if he had a headache while DI Davies had a look of doubt and suspicion. Jill interpreted the men's emotions and said, "You're giving us a look as though we're spinning you a story about your local legend, King Arthur. Contact Special Agent Leticia Ortiz of the FBI's office in San Francisco, CA in the United States or Belgian Police Inspector Willems in Brussels and they will verify our story and credentials.

Nick was a good friend and we'll go to work on solving his murder, and we would rather work with you than separate from you."

DI Jones stood up saying as he exited, "I'll go check those references."

DI Davies looked at the women and said, "Tell me more about Nick Brouwer. We need to notify his family. Did he ever mention parents or siblings or a spouse?"

The women looked chagrined and shook their heads. Then Marie said, "We probably spent a total of ten days around Nick over the two years and I can't ever recall him mentioning family." Then looking at Jill she added, "Maybe Nathan or Henrik know about his family, I'll contact Henrik and why don't you drop a text to Nathan since he is likely still asleep at this time in California and it would scare him to get a call at this hour from me. I also think Henrik was closer to Nick."

Angela spoke for the first time, "I knew Nick better than my friends here and he never mentioned family; despite many long telephone conversations between us and questions from me. He never revealed more than he had no immediate family."

Ignoring DI Davies, Marie checked for reception then said, "I'm going to step outside to call Henrik, be back in a few," and she exited the room.

DI Davies was nonplussed. Usually, people brought into interview were intimidated enough to request to leave the room. Not this woman, she just got up and left. Americans had a reputation for being bold and he guessed that was what he was seeing. Now he just needed to regain control of the situation.

With patience in his voice he asked, "Who's Henrik and who's Nathan?"

"Nathan is my boyfriend, and Henrik is the husband of the woman we saved in Belgium that was later murdered at the hospital. He's also the CEO of Gunter Industries, a high tech security firm. He, Nick, Nathan and the four of us had a quick vacation about a month ago at his house in Germany."

DI Jones re-entered the room much to Davies' gratitude. He was simply disbelieving of everything the American women were saying.

"I was able to reach both Inspector Willems and your Special Agent in the United States and they both implied I should let you run this murder investigation." He paused and looked around the room, then checked his notes and asked, "Where's Marie Simon?"

"She went outside to make a call to our friend Henrik Klein in Germany," replied Jill. "He was also a friend of Nick's and may know about his family. Besides he deserves to hear of Nick's death from us."

"I think we need to start this conversation over," Jones said. "You'll have to admit your background is very unusual. We've had people in the station before claiming that they could help us on an investigation. Often they're self-proclaimed psychics who do nothing more than waste our time and energy. You ladies seem to be the genuine article, and I'll take the advice of my law enforcement peers in Brussels and San Francisco and ask for your assistance in finding Nick Brouwer's murderer. My first question for all of you is if he was supposed to meet you at the bar, what was he doing at the castle?"

They looked up as Marie returned to the room. She sat down and said to her three friends, "Henrik is devastated by Nick's murder. He said that Nick wasn't worried about anything. As for family, I think he feels as bad as we do about not knowing more about Nick's family. How about if we contact the restaurant owner Max in Amsterdam? Wasn't he an old friend of Nick's?"

Angela sniffed and said, "One problem at a time. Let's solve Nick's family notification first. How about his passport; does he list an emergency contact there?"

DI Jones replied, "He didn't have his passport on him. We'll contact the Dutch consulate to see what they have on record for his passport and see if they can assist us in finding his family."

"If you give me access to a computer," Marie requested, "I'll do a background search on Nick and see if I can find his family. It usually takes me about thirty minutes which is probably faster than the consulate can get you an answer."

"Nick was a member of the Dutch police force for about a year and they also might have information on him," Angela suggested. "You could also check with his company, although I don't remember him ever telling us what the name was of his security company. I'm having a hard time believing that I know so little about him."

She got looks of sympathy from her friends as there had been the faint hope that Angela and Nick might evolve into a romantic relationship once they conquered the distance barrier between the two of them. Now there was only a fantasy of what might have been.

DI Jones asked Angela, "Were you involved with Mr. Brouwer?"

Angela paused searching for the description of the relationship and finally said, "Yes… in a way. We weren't a committed couple as we hadn't figured out how to bridge the distance gap between Amsterdam and Green Bay, but Nick was exploring the option of expanding his company to the United States which would have at least put us on the same continent."

In the silence that followed Angela's remarks, Marie could be heard to be busily typing away on a laptop supplied by the DI. Jill and Jo focused on the murder. Why had Nick gone to the castle and who had he angered enough to find himself dropping off the edge of a castle wall?

"What can you tell us about the murder scene?" Jill asked. "Did anyone see someone push Nick over the edge? Did they hear any conversation? How tall was the barrier in front of him? What's your guess as far as the size of the murderer? Could a woman have pushed him over the edge?"

"Whoa, that's a lot of questions. Our crime scene unit is over at the castle collecting data from the murder scene. I'll have answers for you in a few hours," replied DI Jones.

Marie looked up and said to her friends, "I can't believe we've never searched Nick's background. We just trusted him from the moment we met him. Now that I'm looking into him, he appears to have a few holes in his background."

"Like what?" asked Jo.

"He appears to have been born perhaps six months before we met him," Marie said. "Not literally of course, but there's no record of schooling, relationships, or even serving the police. I'm wondering if he's even a native of the Netherlands. Since he traveled here by train, he wouldn't need a passport which is a good thing since there's no record of anyone by that name having a passport in the Netherlands. It looks like our first task in this murder investigation is figuring out who Nick Brouwer was since he doesn't appear to be the person we thought he was. I'm not saying he was connected to anything illegal or he was doing anything criminal, it's very odd that he doesn't seem to exist as a human being."

There was silence in the room as the women thought back to their interactions with Nick over the past two years. They tried to think of any information he revealed about himself during those conversations and came up blank. His background appeared mysterious, and yet they who chased mysteries all the time hadn't seen or delved into it.

"Doesn't he run a hotel security business?" asked Jo. "Is he still managing the security of the hotel we stayed at in Amsterdam? Can you trace Nick's background by his business ownership?"

"Good questions. Give me a moment while I research them." Marie replied.

The two inspectors were somewhat bewildered by the

women's approach to the murder investigation. It was like they were not even in the room and they just took off investigating any direction that came to mind about the murder victim. Not that they had disagreed with the direction the women had taken, and to be fair, both contacts in the FBI and Interpol had warned Jones to expect this behavior.

CHAPTER 2

"Let's slow down a moment and plan out this investigation," Jill suggested. "Inspectors, what do we need to do to make sure that you'll share with us any findings on this case? As you know, we can be a real help but only if you agree to a mutual sharing relationship."

DI Jones gave Jill the squint eye and asked, "What do you mean by a mutual sharing relationship?" he asked the question with a frown on his face and a hand rubbing his temple. Jill wondered if this is how he looked whenever an investigation wasn't going the way he envisioned.

"This is what I think we should do," Jill replied. "I've got nearly two decades of experience as a medical examiner. I'd like to join your medical examiner during the autopsy. I think you should take Angela to the castle and let her photograph the crime scene and talk to anybody that might have witnessed Nick's fall. Jo and Marie can best serve the Welsh police and Nick by doing computer searches. If you'll share any information you already have and any news that comes your way as we will with you; I think we'll find Nick's murderer faster."

DI Davies still hadn't gotten his brain around a potential role that these women might play in his investigation. The Welsh police department had never used civilians to assist them formally in solving crimes. On occasion they used informants, but they had never so much as hired a private detective from Cardiff to help them with a case. Furthermore, he had this feeling that the women would at best, solve the murder before them, and at worst get harmed by the murderer. He and Jones needed to step out of the room and discuss how they were going to incorporate these new and unique resources into their case.

"Ladies, would you mind if DI Jones and I step out of the room?" Davies said. "As you can imagine we've never been offered the use of private investigative services before and I think we need to discuss privately how we can use you and yet still stay within the policies of the Welsh Police Department."

The two Inspectors left the room, and the women just shrugged and moved on to discussing Nick's death. Jill heard her phone sound with an incoming email. She looked at it and said, "Nathan's awake and he also does not recall Nick mentioning any family. He also asked if we need him to arrive a few days early."

Nathan had been planning on joining them in Edinburgh. While Jo, Marie, and Angela flew back to the United States, Nathan and Jill were staying two additional days to visit two wineries in Scotland as well as some distilleries.

"We don't need him here at the moment and it's not like Nick's funeral is going to happen before he originally planned to land in Scotland," Marie noted. "So I would tell him to meet us as planned in a few days."

Angela and Jo nodded their agreement to Marie's suggestion. Jill took a moment to reply to Nathan, then settled into the case. She asked Marie to look up the murder and autopsy rates in Wales. The murder rate was low but autopsies were performed on about twenty percent of all deaths, so Nick should be in good hands here. Besides it wasn't like his cause of death was hard to identify, falling some distance off a castle wall would result in brain damage, possibly a broken neck, and potentially the break of over two hundred other bones in the body. Maybe his body would contain scars, markings, or tattoos that might identify who he was or where he'd come from.

DI's Jones and Davies returned to the room resuming their seats. Jones said, "Our Assistant Chief Constable is going to join us in a few minutes. We'd like to set some ground rules with you."

The women nodded in agreement. While they were waiting, Jill decided to ask a few questions of the detective inspectors.

"How many murder investigations have you closed? I wouldn't think that you have a high homicide rate here in Wales."

DI Jones replied, "I've been on the force for close to twenty years and a detective for the past ten. You are correct that we don't have many murders in Wales, I've probably closed around thirty murder cases over that decade."

Jill looked over at DI Davies who replied, "I've been his partner the entire time."

Thirty cases was a solid track record for murder investigations, Jill thought. Nick should be in good hands.

"Have you had many unsolved cases?" Angela asked, anxious to hear validation of their great detecting abilities.

"Over the decade perhaps one or two at most. As with your country, many of our homicides are linked to drugs and gangs and they leave evidence of their criminal behavior."

The door to their conference room opened and a woman in uniform walked in. They didn't know what the stars on her uniform meant, just that she had a lot of them, so that likely indicated that she was the Assistant Chief Constable that they had been waiting to arrive.

The woman held out her hand as she said, "Hello I'm Assistant Chief Constable Lily Morgan. Would you introduce yourselves and tell me about your investigative skills."

Jill took the lead introducing herself and her teammates while describing each of their particular skills. With the introductions complete, Jill hoped this would be the start of the Welsh police cooperation going forward.

ACC Morgan said, "I understand you've been friends of the victim for about two years and yet we're not sure if we have his real identity or if he has any family. That is most unusual, and I can't think of a prior case in Cardiff that began like this one. We on rare occasion have a dead body that we can't identify, but that is usually due to the degradation of the body; however, that's not the case here.

"I also understand that you're asking to be active participants in our investigation and that DI Jones has verified your helpfulness with both the Belgian police and your own FBI. We have never used resources such as yours in any other case of the Welsh police."

Great, Jill thought, they were not going to be allowed on the inside to solve Nick's murder. It would take them so much longer to solve the case without the help of the Welsh police.

After a pause, Morgan continued, "I'm all about trying new techniques to solve terrible cases and so we'll include you in our investigation. I believe you called it mutual sharing. I would like to get a verbal confirmation from the four of you that you'll share information immediately with the Welsh police and you won't share any information with anyone other than us."

The four women nodded and verbalized their agreement with the ACC's requirements. She nodded back to them and left the room. DI Jones directed the conversation.

"Dr. Quint and Ms. Weber, if you would like to accompany me, we'll head to the crime scene as our techs are wrapping up their evidence collection. An autopsy is scheduled for tomorrow morning, and after we visit the crime scene, we'll make arrangements to get you to the Coroner's office in the morning. Ms. Simon and Ms. Pringle we can set you up with computers here or perhaps you would like to work at your hotel."

Jo and Marie looked at each other, read the answer in each other's eyes, and then Marie said, "Could we check out two laptops from you to work at our hotel?"

"I think I can arrange that, give me a moment," replied DI Davies and he left the conference room.

Jill was concerned for Angela as she and Nick had a deepening relationship for the past two years and she'd hoped that this might be the year that Angela and Nick could work out a long distance relationship. They all liked and respected Nick, but Angela was the one that 'liked' Nick the most. At least when they visited the crime scene, his body should've been removed and Angela wouldn't have the opportunity to view Nick dead. The friends split up and went in two different directions to help with the investigation.

Angela and Jill followed DI Jones outside to his car, a Ford Focus in royal blue and fluorescent yellow with the word "Heddlu" in bold letters with "Police" underneath. Welsh was one of six Gaelic languages and Welsh schoolchildren were required to learn the language in school. Thus every sign they'd seen was bilingual. There was no cage between the front and back seats, so Angela asked, "How do you protect yourself from criminals in the back seats of your cars?"

"They don't ride in these cars; we call for a transport van if we need to move a criminal and it has a cage inside of it."

"Are those transport vans busy all day? Do you transport many people? What do you do with drunks?"

"We don't have as many crimes here as in your States. Many of our drunks go to A & E at the hospital rather than jail."

"Is that working?"

"Is what working?" Jones asked.

"Are your alcohol-related incidents higher or lower than the rest of the UK or Europe?"

"We don't have the answer to alcohol or drug abuse if that's your question. Nothing seems to work from my perspective. We even tried cameras in bars recording people that behave like idiots while intoxicated and that offered no deterrent to drinking."

They arrived at the service entrance to the castle and were waved through by security. The castle appeared deserted with few people walking around. Jill checked her watch and noted that it was close to closing time for the castle, but then again the police had probably ordered the castle closed to aid in the collection of evidence at the crime scene.

"Where exactly did Nick fall from at the Castle?" Jill asked.

"The summer smoking room at the clock tower," replied Jones.

"Were there witnesses?" Jill asked. "I would think during regular visiting hours, that there would be a lot of witnesses."

"There were witnesses to his falling but no witnesses in the summer smoking room from where he was pushed out the window."

Both Angela and Jill closed their eyes thinking about what it was like to watch such a fall. They'd visited Cardiff Castle perhaps an hour before Nick's murder. Jill was certain that she would have nightmares if she witnessed such a fall. Sure she'd come close to violence both as a pathologist and from being close to murderers in some of their recent cases. As she got older, she was starting to fear heights and the thought of falling from the distance of the tower just made her shudder on so many levels. The sheer panic while you were in the air before hitting the ground. The desire to grab onto anything before you landed, and the massive pain in the seconds before you're unconscious. It was one of those questions experts would be unable to answer; if you fell and broke all of your bones how long were you conscious after impact?

Jill put the thoughts out of her mind. There was no reason to dwell on the question as it was unlikely that any scientific study would ever be undertaken to provide an answer to the question.

DI Jones parked next to other police cars and exited the vehicle. Jill and Angela had stood in the summer smoking room and close to the base of the tower where Nick landed during their castle tour. Now they approached the ground where Nick landed and they could see mostly dried blood where his body came to rest. They stood looking up trying to grasp how Nick had fallen.

"It appears he struck that roof on his descent to the ground," Jill said while pointing toward another blood stain on the roof.

"That is what our crime scene staff determined as well," replied Jones.

Angela was looking pale after looking at the blood stains, and so a concerned Jill asked, "Do you have your witnesses sequestered somewhere? Perhaps we could take Angela there to begin interviewing the witnesses."

Jones looked at Angela, noted her pallor and understood why Jill wanted to move from the crime scene. He was surprised, as these women had been involved in several high profile murder investigations. Then he mentally shrugged and concluded that the other murder cases had not focused on a friend. He walked the two women over towards a castle office and found his constables and witnesses in a series of empty rooms behind the public areas.

After talking to one of the officers he came back to where the ladies were standing and said to Angela, "Our constables have interviewed about half of the witnesses. We're going to gather them together and introduce you as an expert consultant, and then you can start at the beginning interviewing them."

Angela nodded and then said to Jill, "I don't have any paper, do you?"

Jill shook her head and said, "I don't have any either."

Angela looked over Jill's shoulder to the gift shop behind her where it appeared that a salesperson was counting money getting ready to close for the day. Jill turned and then looked back at Angela with a nod to follow her, and they walked into the gift shop. Sure enough they found some castle stationary that they could use to take notes. Minutes later, purchases in hand, they were ready to begin the interviews.

Jill watched as Angela entered the first room, resolute to help them find Nick's killer with terrible grief just under the surface. Angela took a shuddering breath to begin her interviews, and she turned and followed DI Jones back to the crime scene.

CHAPTER 3

 ill studied the exterior of the tower and took pictures. Then she was ready to go inside and examine where Nick had been pushed out the window to his death.

"How many entrances, both public and private are there to this building?" Jill asked.

"At least six entrances on three different levels of the building. We haven't completely mapped the castle out yet," DI Jones replied.

"Do you have any video that shows Nick buying a ticket and entering the castle grounds?"

"My crime scene techs have collected all security tapes from the castle."

"How about other camera coverage? Do the businesses across the street have store cameras that face the castle grounds? Have you asked witnesses and employees for any pictures or videos they took of the scene?"

"My techs are taking care of that as well."

"Can we watch any of the footage? I would like to understand how Nick entered the castle grounds - through a public or private entrance. Was he covert in his actions to meet his murderer or was this some whacked visitor that pushed him during a fit of insanity."

"Fit of insanity? Is that an American cop term?"

"No, it's my term to describe when some perfectly reasonable individual turns and kills someone. There is no way to describe it other than insanity."

"I have to agree there. I'm still dumbfounded when I interview rational individuals that commit crimes. I wouldn't call it insanity; to me, it's like their brains exit their head. Let's go over to my crime scene techs to see if they have the answer to your question on how your friend entered the castle."

DI Jones spoke to an officer asking where the security camera room was and soon they were traveling a series of corridors until they arrived at a security office. Inside was a monitoring person from the castle and an officer from the Welsh police, and they were sorting through video footage.

Jones performed introductions and then asked, "Do you have footage of the victim's entrance to the castle? Did he buy a ticket and enter through the public entrance?"

The two men responded they hadn't looked for that footage; they were merely making sure that no footage was lost or recorded over.

"Can you pull up the footage of the public entrance in the thirty minutes before Nick's death?" Jill asked.

They did, and they looked for Nick on the video. After getting a description of what Nick was wearing the four of them watched as the film was fast forwarded. They didn't see him in the footage. She then asked for the same footage of any other castle entrances, and there were four – one was the employee entrance, and the other three were maintenance doors cut into the castle walls. A quick review of the employee entrance yielded no view of Nick.

"Finding where Nick entered this castle is going to take some time," Jill observed. "Let's make sure we have the last twenty-four hours of castle visitors on tape."

The crime scene tech nodded his agreement and DI Jones and Jill left the security room to head to the tower. As they walked up to the summer smoking room, Jill was checking for cameras along the way.

They reached the room, and Jill's eyes went immediately to a broken window through which the wind was blowing. She paused a microsecond and said a quick and silent prayer for Nick. She had a sense of the pain of the broken glass and the seconds of panic as he fell to his death. What an awful way to go, she thought as a shiver ran through her while her eyes teared up. Taking a deep breath and reminding herself that she could grieve later, but first she owed Nick her best focus on finding his killer.

Jones must have sensed that Jill needed a moment to regroup as he stood near the broken window in silence staring out at the grounds of the castle. After a moment Jill joined him at the window and looked out and down.

"I'd hate to be the tourist that watched Nick fall. I'd have nightmares over that," Jill said. Then looking around the room, she pointed to a camera and asked, "Is that the only one in this room?"

Jones studied the room and then agreed with Jill's assessment, "Yeah."

Jill added, "Nick is, was tall; I think about six feet two inches or almost two meters, so I think his murderer was at least as tall and strong. Nick trained in martial arts. Perhaps someone snuck up on him - caught him by surprise. I simply can't imagine Nick just standing there and letting himself be pushed out a window to his death. Maybe we'll get some information off the camera, but since it's aimed away from this part of the room, I don't know if we'll see what happened."

DI Jones, looking around the broken window mused, "Based on our witness statements, Mr. Brouwer didn't jump; he came through the window with arms cartwheeling like when someone has pushed you from behind. I agree that given his skills as you've described, that he should have been able to move out of the way of the average criminal."

"This looks like antique glass. I wonder if it's stronger or weaker than today's glass? With the decorative lead, I would have thought stronger."

"Many of the windows were redone in the 18th century before the creation of plate glass, so while the individual panes are stronger than plate glass; unless it was safety glass, a body of a fourteen stone man would break it."

"You know a lot about glass DI Jones," Jill said.

"My father retired from being a window installer, so I know more than your average cop on that topic."

"Ah, that makes sense. What will the castle maintenance do with this window? Can they recreate historical glass?"

"They'll put modern glass in place for now while their maintenance crew contracts with a historic glass maker to make the original repair. They'll have the window repaired as soon as we take down the crime scene tape."

"There isn't much to be learned here other than Nick's murderer had to be large enough to get him through that window with force," Jill concluded. "I'm anxious to study all of the security footage from the castle. Did you fingerprint this area?"

"I agree about the evidence in this room. Our crime scene techs debated fingerprinting this area, but with thousands of visitors each week, I think we could waste a lot of time running down prints from people that are not the murderer."

Jill nodded, and they turned to leave the room, but then Jill stopped and paused a moment looking around.

"How did the murderer keep the public out of this area? I would think that during the open hours of the castle that someone would always be taking pictures of this room."

"That's a good question, Dr. Quint. As I wasn't first on the scene, I'll get that answer from my men."

"Are there any other ways into this room?" Jill asked. "Perhaps a secret elevator, or maintenance back stairway?"

"Let's look as I don't have the answer to your question."

They each took a side of the room looking for any hidden doors that might lead to another exit to the room. Sure enough, DI Jones found a panel in a corner that moved to reveal a very industrial looking set of stairs.

"Must be that maintenance corridor that you were looking for," Jill said. "It's very industrial looking and has no castle charm."

DI Jones entered the corridor after asking Jill to stay at the top and followed the steps downward. Sure enough after winding through four or five sets of steps, he arrived at another back corridor of the castle on the ground floor. He was breathing heavy once he'd returned up the stairs to Jill.

"The stairs lead to non-public areas that include space for cleaning and maintenance. I didn't notice any cameras on the stairs," Jones said while he looked at the single camera monitoring the summer smoking room. "This doorway may be on that camera, so we'll get a look at which way they came."

"One more question," Jill said. "Can you enter this room without a key?"

Once the stairwell door was closed, Jones tried and failed to get into the room from the stairway.

"Must be a one-way doorway; you can get out of this space in case there is a fire, but you can't get in it from the stairs without a key."

Jones nodded, and they departed the room where Nick was pushed to his death. Jill knew that she could never again visit this castle no matter how many future trips to Cardiff she made. This castle was forever off her bucket list.

CHAPTER 4

Angela wanted to go to the closest Catholic Church, and light a candle and say a prayer for Nick's journey into the next world. She hoped he would have a chance to meet her father and sister who were already in heaven. When she had time later, she would head to St. David's church for a private spiritual goodbye to Nick. All she could do at the moment was try and find who killed him and why. As one of her friends said earlier, how strange that they had never researched Nick as a friend; they simply accepted him. Now none of them knew who he was and she realized that empty space inside her head was also causing her grief.

DI Jones had introduced her to DI Oliver Thomas who had the job of collecting witness statements. It wasn't peak tourist season; still, they had about twenty witnesses between people that were in the castle and those on the grounds that saw Nick's fall. There were more visitors in the castle than that, but these were people that saw or heard his fall. DI Thomas had interviewed most of the people, and some had even been released back to their homes or hotels. The four that remained for Angela to speak with had been close to the fall on the ground or the summer smoking room.

Angela was introduced as a visiting expert consultant on the case and sat down with the two people that had watched Nick fall. Trying and failing to set aside her personal feelings for Nick she paused to get her emotions under control and said, "Tell me what you saw."

The couple looked at her in surprise, probably due to her American accent, and then the woman held out her camera and said, "Mark and I were staring at the tower discussing what we wanted to be framed in our photograph. I was looking at the camera screen playing with the zoom. We both gasped when we heard the man yell as he was falling. I took a few shots out of reflex. I'm sorry."

Angela reached over and placed her hand on the woman's and replied, "I'm a photographer as well and I know what it's like to play with your camera to get that perfect picture. I often snap several frames knowing I can edit later, so I understand why you reflexively shot those pictures. May we see them?"

The woman turned the camera on then looked for the pictures. There were three. Angela and DI Thomas viewed the pictures and then he said, "Ma'am, I'm sorry but I'll need to take your camera and download those pictures. We should be able to return it to you tomorrow."

She sighed but nodded.

Angela swallowed and said, "Tell me about the sound you heard. Did you hear any conversation come from the tower prior to the man's fall?"

"No ma'am."

"Did you see the window break?"

The woman shook her head and replied, "No I was peering through my camera screen."

"I saw the glass break as a man was pushed out the window," replied Mark.

"Why do you think he was pushed?" DI Thomas asked.

"He was reaching back toward the window as though trying to

grasp something on his way out. He also opened his jacket as though trying to slow his descent to the ground. It was heart-breaking to watch as he so clearly wanted to live by the few seconds of action that I saw him make."

Angela took a deep breath and a big swallow and continued with her questions, "Did any face appear in the glass window after the man's exit?"

Mark thought for a while and then said, "I don't recall seeing a face," and looking over at his partner said, "Honey do you recall seeing a face in the window?"

She shook her head 'no' and then spent another moment studying the pictures she took of Nick's descent. She did not see any face in the window in any of the pictures that she took.

"Did you see anyone run out of the tower building?" asked DI Thomas.

"No. We just stood there in stunned silence. We didn't go over to the man to see if he needed help because he made such an awful sound when he hit the ground that we knew he couldn't be alive."

Angela and DI Thomas asked a few more questions but got no useful information out of them. They moved on to the couple that had been inside the castle at the time of Nick's altercation with the unknown subject.

Again introductions were performed and DI Thomas took them through what they had observed. The new piece of information they picked up from that interview was the gender of the assailant. The couple heard two male voices speaking prior to the sound of breaking glass.

"Were they speaking in English?" Angela asked.

There was a pause as the couple thought about the voices.

"I would guess German or Dutch, but I'm not a language expert," replied the man.

"What was the tone of their voices? Were they arguing, or pleasant?" DI Thomas asked.

Again the couple thought for a while, then replied, "Their

voices were soft like they were trying to keep their conversation low. Then there was a burst of words, followed by noises of a scuffle, then we heard breaking glass, and then nothing."

Angela screwed her eyes up for a few milliseconds thinking about Nick's last minutes. Then she convinced herself to snap out of it and move forward to help find his killer. She focused on the conversation, but she could think of no further questions.

Looking over at DI Thomas she said, "I can think of no further questions."

"Mr. and Mrs. Hughes, did we get your contact information? You sound like you're from England, do you live there?" DI Thomas said.

Mrs. Hughes smiled and said, "Yes we're from a little village called Marlborough just down the M4 and we left our mobile number with someone else from your department."

"Thank you Mr. and Mrs. Hughes, for your help," and Angela and DI Thomas directed the couple towards the exit.

DI Thomas checked in with his partner and they all met up in a castle courtyard. Jill placed a hand on Angela's shoulder trying to give her silent support. After discussing their findings, and a promise to send Jill the tapes from the castle cameras, the two women were dropped off at their hotel by the detectives. They scheduled a meeting the next day to discuss developments overnight as well as to make arrangements for Jill to attend Nick's autopsy. Minutes later the four friends gathered in one of their hotel rooms.

CHAPTER 5

"Angela, how are you doing?" Jo asked when Jill and Angela entered the hotel room.

Angela smiled sadly and replied, "I'm okay. I'm going to go to the closest church and light a candle for Nick. Jill can catch you up on what we learned at the castle," and she left the room.

Marie looked at Jill and said, "Should someone go with her?"

"She's safe walking the streets here and I think she'd like to be alone with her thoughts," Jill replied.

The three friends looked at each other and agreed. Perhaps the best thing they could do for Angela was find Nick's killer.

Jill asked Marie, "Did you find out who Nick Brouwer was?"

"Not yet and I'm amazed the four of us never looked into his background before now. If he was a suspect in a different case we'd be ducking all the red flags flying at us," Marie replied.

"He helped save our lives on numerous occasions so regardless of who he is or isn't, he's always been a friend of ours," Jo declared.

"I wonder if Henrik knows anything about Nick. He's more protective of his security and privacy than we are; I wonder if he looked much into Nick's background?" Marie questioned.

"Let's see if he's available to talk with us now," Jill suggested.

After a nod from the others, she put her phone on the table between the three of them and dialed his number. It was answered after only one ring.

"Jill, have you caught Nick's killer? What can you tell me?" Henrik asked, concern coming across the phone line.

The three friends looked at each other, with Henrik's questions. He was usually formal in his interactions with them. Now he sounded like he had been waiting by the phone for their call, willing to forgo social conversation to get to the heart of the matter.

"Hi Henrik, it's Jill, Marie, and Jo on this end of the phone. To answer your question, we haven't identified Nick's killer yet. We're calling you to find out more about Nick. We began researching him this afternoon and his background is so far, filled with red flags. Did you ever run a security check on him?"

"No, I never looked into his background. I checked the four of you out since I thought you were connected to my wife's murder somehow, but I'll admit I didn't review Nick or Nathan and now that we have become friends I wouldn't check in to your backgrounds. That seems such an invasion of privacy. Why?"

"Nick doesn't seem to have existed up to about three years ago. We were trying to help the police locate family as none of us could remember a single mention on his part about his own family. That was why we asked you earlier if you knew anything about his family."

"That's strange! As you Americans would say, I sensed that the river ran deep in Nick, but I hadn't explored that feeling. You want me to do a search now on his background? Do you have a picture of him that I could run through the facial recognition software and see if there's any other name connected with his face?"

"Henrik, at this point we've hit a blank wall. Granted it's very early in our investigation and we usually run into blank walls in the beginning but if you can find anything on Nick that would be great and I'll forward a picture to you if we can find one. I don't ever remember taking a picture of Nick, but maybe he's in the background of one of our numerous vacation photos. Angela is the most likely to have such pictures but she's out of the room at the moment so I'll ask her when she gets back."

"How did he die?" Henrik asked quietly.

"He was having a conversation with someone in a language that was not English, and then there was a scuffle, and he was shoved out a tower window at Cardiff Castle. His landing caused brain damage not compatible with life," Jill said.

There was silence on the phone line while Henrik digested Jill's terrible news, then he said, "At least his death was quick."

"Yes," replied Jill waiting to see if Henrik had any questions or comments.

There was a sigh and then Henrik said, "Well I guess I better get to work helping you find his killer. Send me the photo when you get it."

After the call ended the three women were sitting staring at the phone on the table as if in a trance. Then Marie asked, "Should we take a moment to reroute our vacation. I'm thinking that this is going to take a while since we first have to identify who Nick is before we can deduce who his killer is."

"Good point, we're scheduled to leave Cardiff tomorrow and we're supposed to spend the next two nights in Manchester before heading for Scotland. We don't have train reservations, but we did book a hotel in Manchester," Jill said then looking at Jo asked, "What are the cancellation procedures and I guess we better see if we can stay here a few more days."

By the time Angela returned they had rerouted their trip for the next two days. They were all hoping to get to Scotland, but solving Nick's death was important. Angela agreed with by-passing Manchester and heading straight for Edinburgh. They knew from past investigations that there generally wasn't anything they could do by being on the scene other than having a stronger relationship with the local constabulary, so they could take the train to Scotland and still work on solving Nick's murder.

Angela described her interviews with the witnesses to Nick's fall.

"So there was an argument in a language we can't identify, then a scuffle, and then Nick was pushed out of the tower," Jill noted. "We know the murderer is a male and of sufficient size and strength to shove Nick out the window. I think our next step is to get a copy of the video from the cameras covering the castle."

"Do any of those cameras capture voice?" asked Marie.

"That's a good question I didn't think to ask the video guy if any of their cameras recorded sound, let me ask and also find the time when the tapes are supposed to be delivered here. We may just want to go to dinner now and then come back to the hotel and do some work," Jill suggested.

Jill got a delivery time of one hour for the video footage from DI Jones and so the women left for a pub seeking Welsh food and beer. Jill and Marie opted for shepherd's pie, while Jo was adventurous with cockles, a type of clam. Angela, never one to have an enormous appetite, was having trouble finding interest in food given the horrible day. Knowing she needed something to feed her brain, she settled on cheese and bread.

After dinner, they arrived back at their hotel to find a flash drive waiting for them with the video footage from the castle at the reception desk. Jill had her laptop with her that contained the software from Henrik's facial recognition program.

"There's a lot of footage here and I was thinking about how to divide it up?" Jill said. "Why don't we use Henrik's software to find specific objects? Angela, do you have any photos of Nick that we could use as one of the objects?"

She thought for a moment and then remembered the photos she had taken at the ski resort when her real intent was to identify other people in the bar. Those photos contained a picture of Nick.

She didn't have those photos with her and so spent some time accessing her data cloud where she stored photos. As a professional photographer, she had over a hundred thousand photos on the cloud. After thinking about her filing system, she was able to locate the photo of the group from Colorado. She thought it was the best full-faced picture she had of Nick. She hadn't realized he'd done such an excellent job avoiding being in any photos. Perhaps this was further evidence of a secret life he led. She quickly edited the picture so they had a single headshot of Nick which she emailed to Henrik. Entering the picture into her copy of the software, she started the search for Nick on camera. Five minutes later they had their matches.

They were able to track Nick's approach to the castle and his purchase of an admission ticket at the information booth. He then seemed to walk the grounds of the castle visiting the Roman ruins before pausing to read a text. From there, he strode toward the tower and his eventual death. He was seen entering the tower, but not falling out. It seemed that no camera focused at the front façade of the tower. That was too bad, not because they wanted to watch Nick fall to his death, but rather they hoped to see his murderer peering through the broken window.

"We have Nick's movements tracked and I'm going to let DI Jones and Davies know of our progress. Let's isolate all the pictures of adult males on the grounds thirty minutes before Nick's death. I have no idea how many people that will be – perhaps thirty or perhaps one hundred, but let's see what we get," Jill said.

The next search, because it was so broad, took a lot longer. In the interim, DI Jones requested to visit their hotel to look at their evidence. The Welsh Police did not have the speed and accuracy of the software that Jill had used and hadn't made any headway in tracking Nick's movement in the castle. Their hotel room was small; so they met the detective in a nook area of the hotel lobby.

It was secluded, and it would allow them to keep their conversation private.

Just as they saw DI Jones approaching them, Jill's laptop pinged that the second search was complete. The detective had a mixture of emotions on his face. He appeared to be anxious and excited to look at their findings, but there was chagrin that his department lacked the software that Jill had so easily used. He had pride that his department used the latest techniques and technology to solve a crime and yet these amateurs from the United States were proving to provide the quickest leads in this case.

Jill gave a brief overview of the software and how it searched. Pointing to her laptop screen she said, "We see Nick approaching the castle from that direction. We're not familiar enough with Cardiff to guess where he was coming from."

"I'd say he was coming from the train station," DI Jones remarked.

Jill continued pointing at the video and said, "You can see he purchases an admission ticket and then walks around the castle grounds. He looks at his cell phone, at probably a text, and immediately heads over to the tower. We see him enter the tower and that's the last we have of him on video. None of your cameras are aimed at the front façade of the tower."

"That's amazing technology you are using. It would have taken my department hours to collect that same feed that you did in I'm guessing fifteen minutes."

"Yes, I think the technology is pretty special. After this case is over if you'd like more information about the technology, just ask. I did a second search looking for adult males. This will be a lot of faces to sort through. My computer pinged that the report was completed just before you arrived, so I've yet to look at it."

Jill paused and pulled up the results of the search. In total, inside the grounds of the castle, the technology identified sixty-two males for Jill to follow up on as potential suspects. She held her laptop out to DI Jones and said, "I'll begin sorting through these sixty-two males for someone that meets the physical profile to have the strength to shove Nick out a window. I'll follow the path of perhaps my top five candidates based on that criterion to evaluate their behavior. Maybe I'll see a guy sending a text within a minute or so of the time that Nick reads the text on his phone. Can you think of anything else to do with this technology?"

Jones paused a moment thinking about the crime scene, but try as he might he couldn't think of another way to approach identifying the murderer other than the one that Jill was taking. He said out loud, "I can't think of any other way to get a handle on our suspect. I do think he likely surveyed the castle to determine where he wanted to murder your friend so he may have visited earlier in the day or the previous day to determine the perfect spot. Also, we're both focused on men as one of the witnesses heard two male voices; but I think a woman with the right skill set and voice could have been the murderer."

Jill nodded and said, "I know what you mean. I have my green belt in tai chi, and my boyfriend has his master black belt in Hapkido, and there are women in both of those martial arts that can toss a far bigger man out a window using the right mechanics, but I think it makes sense to focus on men first."

Jones nodded and agreed. Jill provided him copies of the footage of Nick's movements as well as the sixty-two males so they could work it on their end and they parted for the night. Jill returned to their hotel room to find that Angela had refined another picture of Nick and forwarded it to Henrik. They went to bed that night with heavy hearts and a deep shadow cast on a vacation that they'd planned for the past year. This trip to the United Kingdom would always be remembered first and foremost by the death of their dear friend, Nick Brouwer.

CHAPTER 6

The next morning at breakfast they discussed their steps on the path to finding Nick's killer. Both Marie and Jo exhausted their angles of the investigation. Jo had been unable to find much more information about his company than they already knew, and Marie without Nick's real identity had found little on the Internet to frame the picture of Nick and his life. Jill was being picked up by DI Jones and Davies to head over to the medical examiner for Nick's autopsy. It was going to be weird as she'd never participated in an autopsy on anyone she remotely knew. She needed to find her detached, clinical mind in order to help Nick best.

Angela, Jo, and Marie agreed to split up the sixty-two males, and within a short time, they had their top five picks for potential murderers of Nick Brouwer. Then it was a matter of putting the five pictures through the facial recognition software to get their identities. A second run was done to see if they were seen entering the tower close to the time of Nick's death. Four of the five names came back positive. Marie and Jo did a background check on the four men while Angela traced the path of the four men through the castle.

Jill was waiting at the curb in front of the hotel when the detectives pulled up. The coroner would be joining them for the autopsy at University Hospital which Jill guessed was where the pathologists were located. She'd read up on the department and felt quite confident that Nick's autopsy was in good hands.

They arrived, and introductions were made before they departed for their respective locker rooms. While Jill didn't expect to get physically involved with the examination, she changed into scrubs just in case any blood or guts landed on her street clothes as those substances would have to stay there until she returned home. She met the detectives in the hallway dressed in protective gowns covering their suits and proceeded into the autopsy suite. Whether she was in Sacramento or Cardiff, the room looked the same with stainless steel tables and sinks and the accouterments of her trade – saws, scales, and a variety of tools to peer inside the human body.

They started with a visual examination of Nick's skin noting scars, tattoos, bruises, and scratches. With the scratches on his face, it pointed to his traveling out the window face first as though he was pushed in the back. This explanation didn't make sense from the witness statements as they reported a scuffle before hearing the sound of breaking glass, but perhaps Nick was surprised by someone sneaking up behind him and shoving him before he had a chance to avoid going out the window.

He also had an old scar on his shoulder that appeared to be a bullet wound. Jill couldn't remember him favoring an arm, so the injury hadn't limited his mobility. There was another wound on the side of his hip that had the appearance of a knife wound. His teeth showed excellent dental care, and then they found an odd tattoo. It was tucked under his hairline in the back, but it was quite detailed. Jill took a picture and sent it to her friends so they could begin tracing the tattoo's origins.

Nothing else was remarkable. The pathologist tested Nick's eyes as it would be used to determine his exact age. Pathologists had discovered that the amount of carbon contained in the crystalline of the eye correlated to age within a year. Since they were at a University, students would perform the testing, and they would have his age within a few hours unofficially. A pathologist would later review the calculation to place his age officially in the autopsy report, but it was additional information to collect and use to identify who Nick Brouwer really was. Nick had many broken bones, and his brain was surrounded by blood – a massive brain bleed caused his death, and a fractured skull. The spinal cord was severed as well so if the brain bleed hadn't killed him the spinal cord injury likely would have. His body would remain in the Cardiff mortuary as they still hadn't found a family to claim him.

Jill exited the autopsy room and entered the locker room to change back to her street clothes. Her thoughts focused on identifying the significance of the tattoo as well as the other clues to Nick's background – prior wounds, proper dental care, and later today they would have an age for him. She had guessed forty-two to forty-eight years of age. They didn't know his real age, name, marital status, and ethnicity. All they knew was that he had defended their lives on numerous occasions and that was enough to chase his killer to the ends of the earth.

Jill met the detectives in the hallway after changing into her street clothes. On their end they were pursuing the real identification of Nick. It was strange how he appeared out of nowhere about eighteen months prior to when they met him for the first time. She had some ideas she wanted to discuss with her friends outside of the listening range of the two detectives. She was also very interested in the tattoo. She'd seen many strange tattoos in her life as a medical examiner. They were usually full of meaning to the deceased, and she hoped that was the case with Nick.

"Was anything different from an autopsy that you performed in the United States?" DI Jones asked.

"No," replied Jill. "The facilities and processes were remarkably similar. I suspect that both forensic science and police science are the same the world over. There are technological enhancements that develop and marginally put one police department in front of the other, but I can say that after my experiences in the various states of America and now with Belgium, the Netherlands, and Wales, that we pretty much all operate the same and under very similar judicial requirements. Gun ownership varies from country to country, but that's about it."

"That would be about my sense of the world," agreed Jones. "What are you doing the rest of the day? What are your plans for staying in Cardiff?"

Jill gave the detective kudos for asking the questions. A good detective would want to know if Jill was pursuing a different thread of investigation from the one he and Davies planned to take.

"I'm going to check in with my friends to see what they've accomplished with the list of males at the castle. I also asked them to work on tracking down the tattoo. As far as how long we'll be in Cardiff, we reworked our vacation schedule to spend additional time here before moving on to Scotland. We'll continue the case from there, but at a certain point in every investigation, there's no need for us to be in the city of the murder. My team uses forensic findings and technology to solve murder cases. We do some first-person interviews, but those always seem to be at the outset of a case rather than an ongoing need. What are you detectives working on?"

One good question deserved another thought Jill. She wondered if the two detective inspectors were pursuing an angle she and her team hadn't thought of chasing.

"Like you, we're tracking down the video faces and tattoo. We also expect results back from our crime lab on the fingerprints we dusted for at the scene and on Mr. Brouwer's body. We've also got our searches going with British intelligence and Interpol to find the identity of our victim."

"Let's keep in contact then, and I wish you good luck with this case, detectives," Jill replied. While they were discussing the case, the detectives had been driving her back to her hotel. A short time later she was reunited with her friends and teammates in one of the hotel rooms.

Angela had enlarged the picture of the tattoo near Nick's neckline. It was surprisingly easy to find information on Google of such a tattoo and once they located the significance of the tattoo that generated furious research into the tattoo's origins by her friends. The source didn't make sense as it pointed to an organization that to the best of their knowledge ceased operations in the early 1990s. Nick had probably been in high school at the time. Since they didn't know his real age yet, it was hard to judge that aspect.

CHAPTER 7

"What are you talking about?" Jill asked her friends.

"Operation Gladio," replied Marie.

"What's Operation Gladio," asked Jill. A quick search of her memory turned up no reference to a word, "Gladio," but it sounded Italian.

"It's an organization that allegedly disbanded in the early 1990s, but it makes for fascinating reading. There's even a YouTube video produced by the BBC on the subject," replied Jo.

"Okay I get that it's something that was supposed to have dissolved in the 1990s, but what is it?" Jill asked frustrated.

"Oh, well it's a spy organization," replied Angela.

Jill's friends all had this look of intense concentration and excitement. Their emotions failed to transfer to her given that she didn't know enough about the organization to be excited about it. She wondered what had flipped the switch for her friends; she couldn't recall this zeal for research in another case. Perhaps her problem was where she'd come from; Nick's autopsy had been very sad for her.

Jo must've caught that glimpse of sadness in her eyes as she patted the seat next to her and said, "Jill, come look at my computer screen and I'll explain. I'm so sorry you had to witness the autopsy of our good friend Nick."

Jill replied, "I've been doing autopsies for nearly two decades and yet today was the first time I knew the person laying on the stainless steel table. I've assisted family members in identifying their dead loved ones, but I had never walked in their shoes before today. Let me get a cup of coffee, and I'll shake these grim thoughts off, and you can tell me all about Operation Gladio."

Jill left the hotel room in search of said coffee, she was joined by Marie a few steps behind her, and she said, "I could use another cup of coffee too, I think we'll be spending hours trying to understand the spy operation. Where're you going for coffee?"

"Sadly, given that we're in the United Kingdom, the closest place with coffee that I know is that McDonald's at the end of the block and much as I hate to admit it, they have great coffee."

"At home, if I can't find a Starbucks for coffee, McDonald's is my second choice," Marie said. They finished the coffee run in silence and soon returned to the hotel room.

Jill sat down and looked at her three friends each sitting with a computer of some sort and said, "Tell me about Operation Gladio."

"I think it would be best if I explained the context in which it was created in the 1940s, then I'll move on to what it is and why it's believed to have been disbanded in the 1990s. That will help you understand why it doesn't make sense for Nick to be involved with this group," Jo said.

Taking a deep breath, she started with the explanation, "At the end of World War II, the United States and Europe were worried about the power of Russia. Essentially it was felt that the far right needed to prevent the far left from taking over the world. The world's governments were paranoid and its military leaders planned for a hypothetical invader, and created a small but invisible army left behind in countries believed to be susceptible to communist forces."

Jill had such a skeptical look on her face that Jo had to pause and say, "I know this sounds crazy, but we didn't live in those times and people that did always feared another World War. They feared a World War III, and they thought the greatest threat was coming from the Eastern Bloc countries. It was a time of the Cold War. France, Belgium, Switzerland, the United Kingdom, and the United States placed very secret Special Forces in these countries to monitor communications and stash arms should they sense threats from Russia. And these left behind forces continued for the next forty years until the Italian Parliament exposed them in 1990. These forces were outside of the control of NATO but rather were believed to be run by the CIA and MI6."

"Maybe I should've gone out for a few shots of whiskey instead of coffee. This explanation is sounding like a Tom Clancy novel with spies and conspiracies, but continue as it's a fascinating story," Jill murmured.

"These secret special agents are rumored to have caused fabricated terror attacks such as a car bomb in Peteano, Italy, and a massive bomb in the waiting room of the Bologna rail station. The theory being that if it looks like a leftist government was gaining power, then these agents on the ground needed to create political diversions to make those leftist governments lose the support of the people."

"Okay, in summation, the super-secret agents were supposed to cause problems for governments appearing to lean to the left so that the world could stay balanced in the view of the United States and Europe by having mostly democratic nations. I can sort of see how this happened. I was amazed the first time I saw the remains of the Berlin wall which the West saw as evidence of a communist East to be feared. I know that families were kept apart for twenty-five years or so while East Germans were confined basically to Berlin and supported by Russia. I always remember how well they did in the Olympics and was amazed that they had such an athletic machine training people for brilliance and yet they sought to confine them inside a wall. It's hard for me to grasp as an American those limits on your freedom. But let's get back to the discussion at hand. I get the creation of Operation Gladio, but why would Nick twenty-five years later, be connected or even have a tattoo representing that organization? Has some new group taken over that symbol?"

"Maybe a motorcycle club or something like that appropriated the tattoo as their logo?" Angela suggested. "Once we figured out the context of Operation Gladio it seems even more far-fetched that Nick was connected to such an organization. However, given that we have no history on him older than three years, then something secret is in his background, but I don't see how it could be this, given the time in history that it occurred."

"Unless the Operation didn't go away," Marie suggested. "Maybe the European and American governments are lying about their spying activities. Actually, they probably are as that's basic for spying 101, I think. Then again what's the need for preventing Russia from taking over the rest of the world? I for one don't feel threatened."

Her friends grinned at her analysis. At heart, they were optimists, unable to understand how people lived by believing the sky was about to fall.

"I think our bigger threats are North Korea or ISIS terrorists; any whack jobs with access to bombs or missiles, but that's neither here nor there," Angela declared.

"Perhaps we should discuss this finding with Henrik. As a German, he may have an entirely different view of Operation Gladio and spying in general," Marie suggested.

"That's a great idea," Jo agreed. "We may be letting our American view get in the way of the truth or at least an understanding of these groups."

Jill looked at the time, it was still morning in Germany, and she had no idea what a high tech CEO might be doing at this time of day. She supposed he'd be in meetings, but they would soon find out as she dialed his number.

CHAPTER 8

"Hello Jill, have you found Nick's murderer?" was apparently Henrik's new way of answering the phone. This told her he had faith they would quickly solve the case and that he was worried enough to drop his usual polite manner of easing into a conversation.

"Sorry, but we haven't Henrik. We wanted to pick your brain to understand a secret operation that began after WWII that Nick may have been affiliated with."

"I don't doubt that he was involved in with some kind of secret as I still have been unable to identify his real identity beyond Nick Brouwer who as you said appeared to have been created three years ago. It's so rare that I can't find the identity of someone and our friend Nick has become a personal challenge for me. Tell me about your secret operation."

"I attended Nick's autopsy a few hours ago, and he appeared to have healed bullet and knife wounds. He also had a tiny tattoo under his hairline. We've identified that tattoo as belonging to Operation Gladio, a secret leave behind army that NATO countries created at the end of WWII. At that time, the fear was Russia would expand its left-leaning philosophies to Europe. Paranoia was rampant, especially after the Berlin Wall's construction. There was fear that Italy would be the next target. Allegedly these armies had their origins in the CIA and MI6, and according to the Italian parliament, these ceased operations in the early 1990s. Nick would have been too young to have any involvement in such a secret army, but we have no other explanation for the tattoo. He was heard to be in conversation with someone shortly before a scuffle broke out and then he was pushed out of the castle tower. Witnesses didn't see the faces of the two men, but we're sure it was Nick and another man. The language wasn't recognizable by the witness but thought to be German or Dutch. Have you heard of Operation Gladio or stay behind armies in Europe?"

There was a pause at the other end of the phone as Henrik was thinking about Jill's words and then he said, "I've not heard of Operation Gladio, but as a German, I've lived through the Berlin Wall. As for stay-behind armies, I'm aware of them, but not the specific one you're referencing. I have a friend who is a political science professor at Stuttgart University. Let me give him a call and pick his brain about stay-behind armies. He sees conspiracy everywhere, so I'm sure he's up to date on these groups. I'll give you a call or email you with what I learn."

"I bet Henrik has some interesting opinions on the Berlin Wall," Marie said. "He's lived through history that we can only imagine. We'll have to ask him about it sometime."

"We had 9-11 in our country and the civil rights movement, but other than that, recent American history is boring compared to other parts of the world," Jo said.

"How about if we spend another thirty minutes searching for more information on Operation Gladio then we could visit the Brains Brewery sample their beers and toast to Nick," Angela suggested ever the beer aficionado.

Her friends agreed, and soon there was silence in the room as they were chasing facts about the operation. Marie was amazed that Facebook had recent comments from people about Operation Gladio; mostly the conversation seemed to be that the Operation had never gone away.

Nick's tattoo only made sense if the Operation was active in say the recent ten years. Maybe the Prime Minister had lied to the Italian Parliament saying it was dismantled when it hadn't been, or perhaps the CIA and MI6 lied to the Prime Minister while secretly continuing the operation. It would be interesting to hear the opinion of Henrik's friend; Jill made a bet with herself that he would say that Gladio was still in operation.

Half an hour later, they'd had their fill of paranoid conspiracy theorists, and so their topic of conversation during the brewery tour was how they could get information on the CIA and MI6 secret operations. After all, they were secret, duh! They'd never tried to research what was alleged to be top-secret information. In the covert world, what was real and what was an illusion?

"How about contacting Special Agent Ortiz in San Francisco?" Jo suggested. "Perhaps a friend in the FBI might tell us about covert operations of the CIA. Let me do a quick search to understand the relationship between the two agencies. If they don't get along, maybe the agent might be more willing to assist us."

"That's an intriguing thought; use one American agency against the other," Jill agreed. "How about our friend David Gomez from our Colorado case last year? He was a pretty good hacker. I wonder if he could hack into the CIA's computer and find out if they say that the operation is still valid."

"That's a great suggestion, but I wonder how dangerous that will be for him" Angela agreed. "However much the FBI and CIA might despise each other, I can't imagine them spilling state secrets to us especially if it is top-secret and they wish for the European Union to remain in the dark."

"Maybe we should put aside this trail and go back to the males on the camera feed. You said you thought you'd eliminated four of the five males that were identified last night as potential suspects. What about the fifth male?" Jill asked.

"We've been unable to identify him, and his progress through the castle is certainly suspect," Jo noted.

"Why is it suspect?" Jill asked.

"I was going to go back and study the footage again, but he appears out of nowhere. One moment he isn't there, and then in the next, he appears in the feed. I don't know how tall those castle walls are, but I think he might have gone over the wall." Marie replied.

"Why don't we ask the detectives if they have reports of people climbing over the castle walls? I don't mean in relation to this male, but as a general rule how hard is it to climb? Are there frequent police reports from the castle or others of people getting into the castle without paying admission?" Jill suggested.

"It's certainly a starting point," Marie agreed.

They were inside a room containing huge stainless steel tanks of beer that was distributed to smaller kegs for transport to bar owners and such, as well as a bottling operation where their retail beer was created. The brewery was the largest in Wales, and you found signs and posters everywhere talking about Brains beer. They were on a private tour they'd arranged before leaving America. Angela had worked all of her bar contacts in Wisconsin to find someone with a connection to this brewery, and they'd felt privileged to go on the tour.

After leaving the bottling area, the tour was over, and they were taken to a local Brains Pub and deposited in a beer garden room where they could taste the many varieties of Brains. Seated, each had a different type of beer, and they clinked their glasses and said in unison, "To Nick." and "May he rest in peace."

They then honored his memory with funny stories involving him. Jill's favorite was the wild ride down a mountain road in Colorado while someone in a big dark SUV was trying to push them off the road. He'd instructed her in such excellent defensive driving she should have known he was a James Bond like spy. In the end, the SUV had succeeded in pushing them off the road, but they landed safely in a prairie with airbag powder all over their faces. Jo's favorite was when he rescued them in the windmill in the Netherlands; he used a fake police siren ringtone to get rid of a guy trying to shoot them with poison darts. Marie and Angela liked the facial expression he'd given them when they chased after Nathan who was pursuing a man that held a knife to Jo's throat. Nathan and Nick had a good time using their skills to subdue the man, and he looked affronted that they would even think he would be in danger. It was very cathartic to remember Nick in this manner and with a final clink of their glasses their private memorial service ended.

They returned to their hotel rooms to spend more time tracking this fifth male to decide if he should stay on the suspect list. They'd gotten an email back from the detectives noting that there were occasional reports of someone scaling the castle walls, perhaps twice a year and usually a result of a guy drinking rather too much alcohol and his friends egging him on to try. Since many of them tried this maneuver in the dark, they often ended up with a sprained ankle on the other side of the wall or the realization that they had no other way to scale the wall back and out of the castle grounds. Okay if the average stupid boy could scale the wall, then it was quite possible that their fifth male entered the castle in this manner and then they could conclude that the fifth male was their suspect. It was an infinitely small coincidence that a guy would choose to scale the wall in the middle of the day as a lark perhaps fifteen minutes before Nick was pushed to his death.

"I think we need to go to the castle and study the approximate position that this guy appears and see how high the wall is at that point. We also might want to get any exterior camera footage from the city or businesses across from the castle," Angela suggested.

Since no one had any better idea, they exited their hotel for the walk to the castle. Along the way, they soaked up the beautiful city of Cardiff and the residents that inhabited it. Jill watched people interacting with each other, while Angela stopped to take a few photographs. Jill was always amazed at the composition of Angela's pictures, but then she should have expected this from someone whose profession was photography. Angela was so skilled that Jill found herself rarely taking photographs anymore; she'd just get a copy of Angela's.

They'd used a map of the castle to ascertain approximately where the man appeared, and so they were on Cardiff's North Road. They stood studying the pedestrian traffic and wall height in this area. None of them were rock climbers, but Angela, the tallest of them, thought that if she had that kind of skill; it would be relatively easy to duck into the shadows of the trees and get over the wall using a combination of the brick ledges or the tree to help. While there was both car and people traffic in this area; a man that was quick could time his approach right and scale the wall with ease or for that matter a person could go over the wall in the middle of the night and wait for daylight hours to appear. Still, it would pay to check cameras around the city. Cardiff had nearly three-hundred closed caption cameras collecting footage around the city, so she'd ask whoever was watching the cameras if they had footage of this particular section of the wall. Hopefully, the trees in the area wouldn't block the view.

After asking the detectives about the camera locations, they learned that there were many hours of camera footage and they would need some way to make it usable. The Welsh Police were going to make a run at consolidating the massive amount of footage. Jill knew they could get help from Jo's friend Jack, a video expert, but in order to have his help, she needed a copy of the footage which the police had declined to release to her so far. Jill and Angela returned to their hotel.

"Let's return to Operation Gladio," Jill suggested. "Can we come up with a recent list of perhaps the last five years of anyone that has commented on this topic?"

"I'm not sure that will help. It's a pretty crazy group of people that comment on this topic. They remind me of the case we had in Sacramento; the anti-government people," Jo replied.

"So are there hundreds of people commenting or just a few?" Jill asked.

"Just a few, but I would classify them as bat-shit crazy as they often remark that Russia is going to take over the world," Jo said. "I guess this is a case of you had to live through the Cold War to understand it. I know a few people who see conspiracies around every corner, but I'm not one of them."

CHAPTER 9

For eighty years, the secret order had played a game of chess with the European continent. The order prided itself on upholding its three values: covert operations, death to communists, and prevent a World War III. Of course, in Latin, the motto sounded much stronger and romantic, but over time the order had moved away from their Latin origins. They still spoke in a coded language; well not a coded language, but rather one that few people outside the order spoke.

In 1944 at the start of the order, in the original meeting of France, England, and the United States, they settled on all the order's communications being in Guernésiais, a rare language from the island of Guernsey which was briefly and resentfully occupied by the Germans in WWII. It was a combination of French, Norse, and English and few people in the world could identify the language upon hearing it. This obscurity made it rather perfect for the order as they could readily teach the language to new members. They had little fear, outside the small population of about fourteen-hundred native speakers on the island of Guernsey, of being understood or even detected as to the language's origin. At times it sounded like French, while other times it sounded like English or Danish. The French could hear the odd word that they recognized, but it would still be hard for them to follow a complete conversation. The order had never had someone intercept their communications.

In the past decade, the order had sustained dwindling numbers and an ongoing conversation as to its role in the current world order. Communism was at play in few countries, and it was not increasing in popularity. It economically seemed to hobble a society from joining the first world. Countries like Russia and China had drifted from communist doctrine into socialism with capitalistic influences. An original list of twenty-five or so countries was now down to five, and those five provided little threat to the rest of the world. The order had not influenced the formation of a single government in the last twenty years.

New members were recruited out of the military, but the present order members were having a difficult time whipping up enthusiasm or even extolling the victories of the past. No new members had joined in the last decade. There was little mission, and the doctrine was out of date with today's society.

Nick Brouwer had been recruited to the order immediately after his required service to the Belgian military. The Berlin Wall had fallen a few years earlier. It had been a heady time as the order had influenced its destruction. Then Nick had become their strongest proponent for the dissolution of the order as he had not seen any relevancy for the group in nearly 15 years. However, one did not voluntarily leave the order. You were killed in action or died by the hand of your fellow order members so that the secret went with you to the grave. This be killed or get killed was the reason the order had not completely shut down, and it was also the reason there were no new members. Why put your life on the line for a cause that wasn't important anymore. With Nick's passing there remained fifteen members of the order; at odds with themselves and the world they inhabited. The last class of recruits had joined following their father or uncle membership.

All fifteen members were meeting in an apartment across the English Channel in Le Havre, France in two hours. The murder of Nick Brouwer caused an irreparable chasm among the fifteen members. They needed to discuss the future of the order and the women in Wales that Nick was set to meet. How much had Nick revealed to the women about the order?

Jill received a reply from Special Agent Leticia Ortiz that she had never heard of Operation Gladio and the FBI had no current information on the subject. The agent suggested that Jill contact the CIA as their agents would be the ones with knowledge of such an operation. It was another dead end.

After a conversation with her friends, she decided to contact David Gomez, an excellent computer hacker from Colorado to see if he could reach into the CIA records. Her FBI contact did not provide her with a contact at the CIA, and she figured she'd go nowhere without someone opening the door for her. So, she'd bypass their front door and sneak in the back.

Jill met David when he hired her to look into the death of his partner on the ski slopes of Colorado. David taught coding in a public school in hopes of steering his kids towards jobs in tech industries rather than a more criminal use of their skills. Jill knew it would take at least a day before David got back to her.

One of the problems the team was having was the historical context of this group. So much of it dated back long before the invention of the Internet, and so many pieces of communication were lost forever. Jill took another look at everything that Marie and Jo had found on the operation.

Jo stood up and said, "Let's take a tour of the National Museum. Besides, I think we got all of the useful stuff on the order, so I'm not sure there's anything more to do."

Marie looked up and said, "I agree with you. I keep seeing the same rhetoric over and over again. Since we're not getting anywhere, let's at least be tourists while we're waiting for others to get back to us."

Soon the four of them were on the way to the Museum with somewhat lighter hearts when they caught the rare Cardiff sunshine while leaving the hotel. It was a beautiful fall day. Dry and unseasonably warm. Trees and flowers still had the look of peak bloom from the summer, but here and there you could see fall setting into the leaves on some trees. It was such a pretty day they decided to change their destination to St. Fagan's Museum as it had many outdoor areas. With some help from hotel reception, they soon rented bikes and were cycling towards St. Fagans. What a perfect afternoon!

They started on sidewalks next to a road with tract houses but eventually came upon the Ely River Trail from which they had great views of the river on their way to St. Fagan's.

"This sort of reminds me of our trip to Zaanse Schans outside of Amsterdam. It was outside of a major city and more of an open-air museum," Angela said.

"I'm amazed you remember the name of the windmill museum and I like our weather better in Wales. As I recall, it was raining and very windy," Marie said.

"I remember your thick red vinyl raincoat not only keeping you dry but repelling poisonous darts," Jill added.

"I remember Nick using a police siren ringtone to scare off the man shooting darts off at us," Jo added with a grin. "He was inventive in our protection, but wide-eyed at our boldness."

They all held out water bottles and jointly cheered, "To Nick".

After a pleasurable tour of the museum, they debated their next move.

"Should we ride to Caerphilly Castle? My GPS says it's ten miles to walk, so that would take us perhaps an hour to get there by bike," Jill suggested.

"That's not a far ride; it should take us less than an hour to get there. Our other choice would be to return to the hotel and get a taxi there," Jo said.

"Let's ride! When will we ever have another chance to see some of this country?" Angela stated.

"We might get lost," cautioned Marie.

"I'm okay with that," Jill mused, and with nods from Angela and Jo, they set off on the adventure of finding Caerphilly. It was an adventure as their instincts were wrong on the road since the United Kingdom drove on the opposite side of the road from America. Despite Marie's concern, they rolled up to the castle about an hour later. They had enough time to tour the medieval castle before their bike ride back to Cardiff.

Throughout the afternoon, Jill had checked her phone for new emails, but none were forthcoming. She was glad they spent their time outdoors rather than banging their heads against a lack of new information. They had enough time to reach their bike rental before it closed and the dim light of dusk began.

CHAPTER 11

The remaining fifteen members of Operation Gladio were seated on chairs or the floor lining the small apartment. The building was composed of reinforced concrete as many were in Le Havre; built since WWII. Long ago an earlier generation had purchased the apartment where it remained behind a curtain of shell companies that had since dissolved. It was utterly soundproof, so the men could raise their voices and not fear being overheard. As happened for the past fifty years, the conversation was conducted in Guernésiais while members represented Italy, France, Belgium, and The Netherlands. Other European countries had once belonged too, but they had died out with their members. Today was the first meeting with every member present in over five years. That previous meeting had been far more crowded. Jean-Louis Agnes looked around the room waiting for all conversations to end. He'd been their leader for the past fifteen years. He was in his early seventies and had joined Gladio almost fifty years ago. Thinking back to the mood when he joined the group, he couldn't have imagined the conversation they were about to have – how to end it.

As silence reigned, Jean-Louis began with the incantation that every meeting began with since their first meeting. The men joined him in saying the words in Latin "By being silent, I protect liberty."

Looking around the room, he said with a weary voice, "I remember when women belonged to this group. Perhaps they have shown more wisdom than us men as we haven't recruited one in some thirty years."

The men were silent both acknowledging his comment and waiting for him to move on to the purpose of the meeting.

"As you all know I called this meeting to discuss the resolution of Operation Gladio. We have had many discussions over the past decade but have been unable to reach a consensus. I am ready to mandate a consensus if we can't reach one today."

Several men looked surprised at his comment and frowned. Never in the history of the group had the commander said he would reach a decision if the men failed to do so. Opinions were deeply divided, and Jean-Louis wondered if the man that killed Nick Brouwer and those who opposed dissolution of the group were ill? How they could fail to see the changing landscape of the world was beyond them, but like Nick, he saw no future for this group other than killing each other. Nicholas had voiced that very comment at their last meeting.

"What do you mean, you will decide for us? That is wrong," said a man who Jean-Louis knew to be opposed to the group's end. "You're just an old man, and you lack the energy to be our leader."

With a sigh, he replied, "Yes I am an old man, but as we have discussed before there appears to be no purpose for this group."

"What about ISIS? We need to protect our countries from them," said another man.

"What have we done in the past five years to protect our countries from the Islamic State?" Jean-Louis asked. "We lack the intelligence gathering abilities to contribute to that battle. Have we had a role in preventing any of the terrorist bombings of our homes? No, because we lack the sophisticated technologies that the major spy agencies have to source those bastards' actions."

"Abandoning the cause is an insult to all the men that went before us. I'm sure they're rolling in their graves over our discussion today."

Jean-Louis looked directly at Girard and said, "They've been rolling in their graves the past ten years over the lack of action by this group and for us falling behind in technology. You don't even know how to turn on the latest in smartphones. ISIS can't be bothered spying on us because we are so ineffective at sussing them out. We were created to prevent the spread of communism, and that's not the threat in the world at the moment, nor has it been since the Berlin Wall fell in 1989. We are irrelevant, and today we either vote to dissolve the group peacefully, or we'll begin an internal war and kill each other. Either way, we'll embarrass our forefathers, but at least we'll be alive to enjoy our freedoms."

"And our role in discovering hidden Nazi treasures?"

"Again, we haven't found a treasure to return to its rightful owner in the past two years," Jean-Louis replied.

"We haven't completed our mission of finding the Nazi gold train; that was one of our founding tasks," Girard said.

"Girard, when have you spent weeks at a time looking for the train? I think we can leave that to experienced treasure hunters. The most recent exploration of the train's location was in Poland, a country we haven't looked in for at least three decades. Perhaps we've been chasing a myth on that one."

"What about the women snooping around Cardiff over Nick's death. Shouldn't we have a plan to eliminate them? We don't want to be publicly exposed."

"We've survived government hearings in Italy, if the Operation is truly dissolved this time, we'll survive any public exposure merely by the fact we will no longer exist, and there is no record of our members."

Jean-Louis looked around the room and silently counted votes in his head. He thought he perhaps had a 70-30 vote to dissolve the group, but the unknown was whether the thirty percent would turnaround and murder the seventy percent. If that were indeed the case, then he and the rest of that larger group would need to take precautions to survive the coming internal war. He knew he had no desire to kill a fellow member.

"Is there any more discussion?" he asked looking around the room. No one raised their hand. It appeared that no more discussion or compromise was on the tip of any tongue in the room.

"Please raise your hand if you think that Operation Gladio should cease at the end of this meeting," Jean-Louis said and raised his hand in the air.

Counting the raised hands, he announced, "Thirteen ayes to end the Operation." Then he said, "Raise your hand if you want the Operation to continue."

"Two votes to continue Operation. As I noted earlier, as the leader of this group, I'm going to move us beyond the impasse and dissolve this group effective immediately." Looking over at the two that voted to continue the Operation, he said, "Gentlemen, our Operation has ceased. Should you wish to continue searching for the Nazi gold train on your own or any other past task of this group, I'll make available to you access to all informants and information that we have. Is there anything else I can do?"

Girard gave him a hateful stare, looked at the other man that had voted with him and stood up to leave the room. He muttered on the way out, "Watch your back."

Jean-Louis sighed for the final time and said, "Gentlemen, I do believe we have a problem. I think Girard sees our vote as a violation of our Founders' creed, but it's a different world than sixty years ago. I think that Girard probably killed Nick Brouwer for his views on dissolving this group and now I believe the rest of us are at risk as well. Suggestions on how to defend ourselves?"

"There are thirteen of us and two of them; it seems like we

shouldn't have let them leave this room," said another member. "We should have taken care of our problem here and now."

"I think we're all hopeful that our dissenters will find cooler heads after their journey to the U.K., or perhaps the police there will capture them, but the thought of shedding blood in this apartment was not on my agenda today," Jean Louis said. "Let's do a daily call-in among the thirteen of us to make sure that any of us that die, do so of natural causes over the next several months. I would advise that you decline all invitations to meet another member of Operation Gladio for fear that our two dissidents are trying to catch you alone. If we notice any further killing of any of us by the two of them, I will do a roll call invite for a meeting of all of us at this apartment forthwith."

After a pause, he added, "I do believe that our only problem is Girard. Giovanni has enjoyed our companionship over the past fifteen years, but he's never killed to my knowledge, and I don't think he has it in him."

There was agreement with his comments and plan as they all wanted to get on with their lives and the idea of constantly watching their backs was unappealing. However, the alternative of killing the two members that day was equally unappealing as no one had killed anyone in nearly two or three decades. They could only hope that as they dispersed far and wide to their respective countries and cities, that Girard and Giovanni would be unable to target them all at once, or instead might be distracted by the women investigating Nick's death.

CHAPTER 12

It was time to head north to other beautiful sites in the United Kingdom. They had rearranged their hotel and train schedule to spend extra time in Cardiff. They felt that they had completed any on-site investigation into Nick's death and now could assist the police in solely an Internet manner. With that in mind, they informed Detective Inspector Jones of their future travel plans. He didn't appear to be sad to see them go. They took two taxis to the train station and set out for Manchester. After spending a day there, they would board the train for Edinburgh, Scotland. Jill had been watching people as was her habit and she was frowning at two groups of people that she could swear she'd seen in Cardiff.

The four friends were sitting across from each other in a four-passenger grouping when Jill whispered "I think I've seen two groups of people on the train with us before in Cardiff. One group consists of a man and woman, and the other contains two men."

"I think I know who you're talking about," Marie agreed. "Angela, you didn't by chance catch them on camera?"

"I might have; describe them for me."

"The one group is trying to act like they're a couple, but in my mind they're lousy actors. He's about six feet tall, pale skinned, unremarkable brown hair, in his late thirties to early forties, slightly on the slender side wearing jeans and a tweed jacket with patches on the elbows. His 'spouse' has black trousers, a frumpy sweater, and a tweed jacket as well. They've been too busy giving us furtive looks to give each other lover like glances," Jill described.

Jo shook her head and in a low voice said, "Once again I missed that we were being followed let alone a single description of anyone in our immediate vicinity. Now that you've tickled my imagination, I'll watch for that group."

Her three friends just smiled at her in indulgence. Jo could walk around the same block when on vacation in Europe and not recognize it. She floated on their travels and missed sights, sounds, and people that the other three women saw as she was distracted by contentment.

Angela had her camera out and was skimming through her recent pictures for people in the background that met Jill's description, but since she hadn't been aware of the two pairs, she focused on getting pictures without people in them.

"I don't have them on my camera; do you remember their clothing so I can be sure to snap them going forward?"

Jill and Marie described the two couples for Angela, and then they discussed what to do next.

"We could get off the train and then get back on the next one coming through the station. If we did it close to our destination, it wouldn't be much of a fare difference," Jill suggested.

"We could get off in Glasgow and spend overnight in that town," Jo suggested. "Is it easier or harder to shake our followers in a small city or a big city?"

"We've never had luck in either type," Marie said.

"How about if we transfer to a local bus in Glasgow and see if they follow us on the bus to Edinburgh. Then we could hop off the local bus one stop short of the main bus depot," Jill suggested.

"We're not exactly inconspicuous with our large American luggage," Angela noted.

"If we do the bus scheme, maybe we could look out the back window to see if we're being followed and if they get on the bus with us we could confront them and see where that takes us," Jo suggested.

The women all privately shuddered at the thought of causing a scene in their own country let alone one in a foreign country.

"How about if we split up with two staying on the train and two heading for the bus in Glasgow. Then both groups will leave our prospective transportation at the last stop before Edinburgh and take Uber to the hotel and meet?" Angela suggested.

Everyone thought for a moment and agreed to Angela's idea. Angela and Jill would take the bus route. That way, Maria and Jill who thought they had each seen their followers would be paired with someone that hadn't noticed. It would take Angela and Jill longer to reach their destination, and they would need Uber to get from Glasgow Central to Buchanan Street for the bus, but Angela looked at it as having an additional opportunity to take pictures. They were thankful that they had Wi-Fi on the train to plan these spur of the moment changes. They would all head to Haymarket, and then take a car service to the hotel in the Charlotte Square area. Making their plans, they gave a unified fist pump while Jill added, "One for all and all for one."

"We sure have adventures whenever we're together now," Marie noted. "Do you think it's karma?"

"I don't know," Jill replied. "Our adventures have brought closure for people wondering about their loved ones. So while it may seem that we attract murder and mayhem, perhaps we're just thrown into the mix to give other people answers."

"I like that explanation," Jo agreed. "We were put here to bring people answers. It helps to be reminded of that; that our lives together have a higher meaning."

"Just think we could be having a boring train ride, but instead we're trying to outsmart some people perhaps wishing to do us harm, I'm looking forward to our adventure in Glasgow," Marie said. "I think Jo and I should get off the train and stretch our legs and then jump back on, just to cause confusion."

"How about our luggage?" asked Jo.

"I think it's safe for the few minutes we're off the train, and if someone takes these seats, we'll move elsewhere in the car. That should help muddy the waters while Jill and Angela actually get off with their luggage."

With the plan in place and Glasgow coming up in ten minutes, Jill and Angela set about taking down their luggage at the same time as the other passengers planning on getting off at that station. Once the train came to a halt, the four got off, with Angela and Jill heading for the exit while Marie and Jo scampered back aboard to resume their seats. Jill and Marie were looking for their four suspects to see what happened. Both carried their iPhone to grab a picture if the opportunity presented itself.

Fifteen minutes later two women were on the train heading for Edinburgh, and the other two were purchasing tickets at Buchanan Bus station for their ride. Jill and Marie had managed to capture pictures of the people following them to share with Angela and Jo. They didn't know if the two men got back on the train, but they lost the other two thanks to their Uber ride. Taxis were in a different area, so they'd been unable to get a ride. If the people tailing them were smart, they'd figure out Uber by Haymarket and have it ready. Angela and Jill high fived each other at their loss of the tail.

Marie showed Jo a picture of the people tailing them, and they watched as people passed through their car but didn't see a match. They debated whether one of them should check one of the other cars for the men, but decided there was no sense alerting them if they were on board. If they weren't on board the train, they were pretty incompetent followers.

"I'm going to send these pictures to Henrik to see if he can identify these people," Marie said. "I can't believe that someone has reason to tail us. Surely they know that we didn't have contact with Nick before his death."

"Just assume they're crazy and then everything makes sense," Jo said with a smile. "What else could we do to lose them?"

"Did you see if the female followed Jill and Angela?"

"No. Why?"

"I thought we could ditch them in the bathroom at Haymarket. Go and pull some clothing out of suitcases so that we're wearing something different. We've both got ponchos and scarfs. Maybe we can make the poncho hood into a hijab with the help of the scarf. Maybe we could add pounds to our frames by putting more clothes on and change from sneakers to boots so that we're taller," Marie suggested.

"You've been watching too many spy movies, but I'm game," Jo replied. "I hope I don't pass out from the heat with all that clothing or freak out with all that stuff around my neck," Jo said mentioning one of her quirks; she couldn't stand to have jewelry or clothing around her neck.

"I hadn't thought of that, but you would only need to keep it on for about ten minutes until we make it outside to our ride."

"I think I can hold it together that long. Can you find a video on how to tie the hijab?"

"I'll text Jill and see if she noticed if the female followed them," Marie said. "Then I'll find a video for us."

A few seconds later Jill answered the text, "Yes she followed us, but we lost them leaving the station, so she might have gone back to the train to get a ride to Edinburgh."

Marie shared her plan with Jill and Angela who were both excited to see how it worked out.

"What do we do about our luggage? We won't be able to change that," Jo asked.

"Good question," Marie replied, and the two women sat in silence wondering how they could cover their luggage. Marie's was black so it was no problem, but Jo's was purple and would stand out.

"Could you cover it with the blanket you bought in Wales?"

"I'll try."

With the game plan in place it was just a matter of reaching the Haymarket station and trying their luck at disguise. Jill and Angela seemed to be in a better position having outrun the people tailing them.

CHAPTER 13

The train pulled into the station, and they had their luggage in hand to get off. They had watched a video on how to wrap a hijab and practiced it a few times to make sure they had it right. Marie and Jo looked around them for their followers but didn't see anyone right away and then they had to keep moving with the flow of people exiting the train and walking off the platform. The two women kept an eye out for 'toilets' to make the changes to their appearance. They located it close to the exit and entered to make changes. They knew they needed to do it fast for the best effect and to be able to reach the Uber stand before fainting from the heat of the extra clothing. They'd taken off their lightweight coats before leaving the train so they had goosebumps upon entering the bathroom.

In under three minutes, Jo and Marie changed shoes, added clothing to bulk themselves up and managed to tie credible hijabs around their faces. With the blanket covering Jo's suitcase, she left first, affecting a limp, and Marie followed sixty seconds later. For not being spies, they thought they had done pretty well. Jo had requested Uber just before leaving the toilet, and it was at the curb waiting when she exited. Stowing her luggage, she told the driver she had a second friend arriving sixty seconds behind her. He was getting antsy as drivers were not supposed to wait long, but Marie walked out of the door and pushed her case inside the car and slammed the door and they were off for their hotel in Charlotte Square. The two women begin pulling off the extra clothing, and the driver looked at them in puzzlement in the rearview mirror. He'd never transported women wearing hijabs who took them off while in the car.

"We thought we were being followed, so we ducked into the toilet and put a disguise on," Marie said.

"Did you call the polis?" asked the driver. "It's just 999 if it's an emergency."

"We didn't call as we weren't sure the people following us meant us any harm. So we just tried to ditch them, and I think we succeeded," Jo said putting her hand in the air for a high five with Marie. "I wonder how Jill and Angela are doing?"

Marie looked at her watch and said, "They won't arrive for another thirty minutes, so we'll have to wait to hear their story."

A short time later they had arrived and were checking into their hotel. Sitting in the lobby was Nathan Conroy, reading something on his phone and sipping a bottle of water. He was the love of Jill's life. He was around six feet tall, slender, black-haired, and a martial arts expert. He was also famous in the wine world for the exquisite labels he created for wine bottles. He'd already checked-in and was awaiting Jill's arrival. She'd been keeping him up to date with their last-minute plan on the train.

He gave a hug to Marie and Jo and said "Go ahead and get settled and come back to the lobby when you're ready. I know there's a pub nearby and we can wait for Jill and Angela there."

The two women were back in the lobby about fifteen minutes later, refreshed and looking forward to a pub. They walked over to it and briefly debated trying whiskey.

"When in Scotland, we should try the local spirits," Marie suggested.

"I haven't been a whiskey drinker since college two decades ago," Jo replied. "But maybe it's time to try it again. Let's ask the bartender for a recommendation unless you know your whiskeys Nathan."

"I'd go with your suggestion and ask the bartender; there are too many distilleries in this country that I have not tried."

The three friends sat sipping single malt whiskey waiting for Jill and Angela to arrive. Jo looked at Marie and Nathan and said, "Wow this is going right to my brain. It's terrific, but if I climb up on any tables and start singing, you'll pull me down before I embarrass the entire United States, right?"

Marie gave her a dopey smile and replied, "No, I'll probably join you on the tabletop, and there will be two ugly Americans breaking glasses with their screechy voices."

Nathan just laughed and said, "I'll sell tickets at the door to your performance so don't expect me to stop any singing and I promise to record it for posterity."

They toasted one another and chatted with the bartender. They were starting on their second whiskey selection when the other two entered the bar.

Nathan was up hugging Angela and then Jill for a more extended hug and kiss.

"Is that whiskey that you're drinking?" Angela asked ready to join them.

"Yes. It's single malt from a distillery in Islay, which is an island directly west of here. I can taste the sea breeze in this malt," Marie said with a grin.

"More likely you've had enough whiskey that your imagination smells a sea breeze," Jill said.

"Hey, our bartender, Andy, said this distillery is on the Loch Indaal which is on the North Atlantic Ocean," Marie said quite proud of herself for remembering the names of the whiskey's origins while holding the glass of amber liquid up to the light.

"Is it tasty?" Angela asked.

"Do we look unhappy with our drink selections?" Jo replied. "This is our second dram and Andy here recommends you drink it neat with a glass of water on the side to help you taste the individual flavors of the whiskey."

"When in Rome," Jill muttered and then looking at Andy said, "I like stuff sweet, so if you have a sweet whiskey I'll take it neat with the water on the side."

"I'll have a Bowmore neat," Angela said.

Her four friends turned and looked at her, and she said, "Hey, I did my research and they're fruity whiskeys. Andy, do you think it's good?"

Andy replied, "You have expensive taste lassie. Some of their bottles go for tens of thousands of pounds a bottle."

"That doesn't sound like your taste Angela," Nathan said.

Angela swallowed and said, "I'd like a dram of their forty-pound bottle. Do you have it?"

Andy busted up laughing and explained to the other bar patrons, "She wants the forty pound bottle."

There was a round of laughter from the men, and two women at the bar and one of them said to Andy, "I want two drams from that bottle too!" and the laughter began again.

Angela said, "Ok, can I have a dram of any whiskey that has a fruity taste in a forty pound or less bottle?"

Her three friends grinned at her and Andy announced to the other patrons, "How about if I give the one that wants it sweet a Laphroaig, and the fruity drinker will get a Glenmorangie?"

There were nods of agreement, and Jill and Angela soon found themselves sipping whiskey. Jo had leaned over to talk to the other patrons, while Marie leaned back in her chair at peace with the world after having too much alcohol on an empty stomach recently fed by adrenaline.

Eventually, they moved away from Andy and the other patrons to talk about what had happened on the train and bus. Marie and Jo went first describing their efforts in creating a hijab. As always,

Nathan sat there uneasy at the risks the women willingly exposed themselves to, but then he silently hit his head with his hand in his mind as he remembered that was part of their charm. He couldn't have it both ways.

"Did that work? Were you followed?" Angela was impressed with their creativity.

"We think it worked; we practiced tying scarfs over the hood of the rain poncho, and the biggest worry was whether Jo would faint from heat before we got into the Uber car. Fortunately, the toilet was near the exit, so we didn't have far to go in all that clothing."

"The Uber driver gave us a strange look when we began removing some of the layers and told us we should call the polis when we explained what happened, which we declined to do. We didn't see anyone follow us, but who knows? We tried to be quick in the bathroom, and we didn't want to look around as we were leaving lest we give ourselves away, but we know for sure that a car didn't follow us," Marie said. "What about you guys?"

"We thought that we were followed out of the train station, but there was no other ride in sight, so we got away unless they later found our Uber driver and questioned him," Jill said. "The bus ride was uneventful other than Angela getting some interesting pictures of heather fields. We didn't see anyone follow us from the bus station to our hotel."

"So what's our next plan?" Jo asked. "Besides drinking whiskey; I'll be needing food soon, or you'll have to wheel me out of here."

"Me too," Marie said. "Let's ask some of these regulars for restaurant suggestions and go from there."

A few minutes later they found themselves at a café a few blocks from the pub. Angela, Jo, and Marie went with a wild Scottish salmon dish, while Nathan bravely tried the Haggis, and Jill settled on Fish and Chips. Everyone was happy with their selection and pleased with the bar patron's recommendations. They were dining in a charming alcove where they couldn't be overheard.

"So ladies what's the latest on Nick's murderer? Jill's been keeping me up to date, but there's nothing like having a question and answer session with you folks to have a real sense of this investigation," Nathan said starting the conversation.

"We've been unable so far to find his real identity or indeed if he has any family. He continues resting at the coroner's office in Cardiff until we can find family," Angela began. "We have two groups of people following us from Cardiff to Manchester and on to Edinburgh. We didn't notice them on the train leg from Cardiff to Manchester, nor did we notice them at the few tourist sites we stopped at in Manchester, but they were following us today on the train."

Marie picked up the story, "We ran into a dead end figuring out who Nick was and any more information on his tattoo representing Operation Gladio. The organization seemed to have died off, and Nick seemed too smart to belong to such a group."

"Except they have this philosophy that you only left the group by death," Jo said. "Maybe he wanted to quit the group, and they wouldn't let him except by death."

"Certainly the unidentified language spoken at the castle before his push to death fits Operation Gladio as one of the documents I read said they spoke in Guernésiais and that fits with what witnesses said. Other than a few people following us on this case we have nothing other than we don't know Nick's true identity," Jill said.

Nathan asked, "Did you find out where the group is based? Is it Italy or France or Belgium?"

"You know I didn't try to answer your question," Marie said. "When we get back to the hotel, I'll work on identifying where their headquarters might be. I don't know if that will tell us anything, but perhaps it will."

"Just a thought," Nathan replied.

Jill glanced at her phone and noticed a new email from Henrik. She ignored the conversation going on around her and opened the email; finally some answers.

"Hey guys, I have an email from Henrik, and he's identified Nick," Jill said excitedly.

"What's his real name?" prompted Angela.

"How did Henrik locate him?" asked Marie.

CHAPTER 14

"His full name is Nicholas Brouwer De Jong. There was no way to find him with such a popular first name without knowing his surname, so at least now we can investigate him," Jill advised.

"How did Henrik find his identity?" Angela asked.

"Henrik said he had an "a-hah" moment as we Americans like to call it. He thought of the several visits that Nick had made to his house and went back and searched security tapes to find the perfect full frontal view of the man. That finally allowed him to be identified," Jill replied. "In all of the other pictures he managed to turn his head to the side and downward."

"It was probably that first visit when Henrik had us kidnapped from Brussels. We were in the dining room for a while, and Nick at some point had to be captured on camera," Angela said as they all thought back to the first time they'd met Henrik.

The others nodded with Angela's description. Their introduction to Henrik had been tense. He'd had them kidnapped off the streets of Brussels and brought to his estate in Stuttgart. They'd all been scared and angry about the kidnapping until they understood that the murder investigation they'd been involved with had

75

been Henrik's wife, a woman he'd loved from the bottom of his heart. Henrik operated a global security company, and they managed to stay in touch in the two years since despite the geographical distance. Henrik's company developed software that was the best facial recognition database that Jill had ever come across. He'd provided her with a free copy for use with her cases knowing that her interactions with police forces across the world would sell additional copies, not that he was in need of additional clients, but business was business.

"Now that we have his identity, could Henrik do a match of his face to public cameras across the UK and Europe to see where he's been this past month?" Jo suggested. "Maybe that will give us a clue as to who had ill will toward Nick."

Her three friends stared at her in wonder.

"What," she asked cheekily. "Good suggestion, huh!"

"That's an amazing suggestion!" Jill said. "OMG, we've made an investigator out of you."

"Well, I've been hanging around with you guys for several years now, and I was bound to pick something up. Just don't think I'll be able to be more observant on the street. I wouldn't go that far in my investigative skills."

There was laughter and the clinking of glasses, then Marie gave Henrik a call to see if he could deliver on Jo's idea.

"Hello Marie, how are you doing? Did Jill receive my email?"

"Hey Henrik, she did, and Jo just came up with a brilliant idea that we wondered if you could carry out."

"Jo?" asked Henrik, apparently puzzled. He remembered the American as brilliant with accounting, and fun, but she seemed to have the least interest in their investigations, and he couldn't ever recall an investigative suggestion coming from her.

"That was exactly our reaction," Marie said with a laugh. "Perhaps she was inspired by the whiskey we've been drinking here."

Henrik chuckled and said, "You Americans are fond of the idea of alcohol-induced creativity aren't you?"

"Hey, it goes back to Hemingway and beyond," Marie replied. "She suggested that you use your facial recognition and the public cameras of the UK and Europe to track Nick's motion in the last month."

"Great idea! I'll have one of my programmers get right on that. I would guess I'll have some information for you by tomorrow morning."

"Great! Nathan's here, and you'll be joining us for dinner tomorrow, right?"

"Yes. I have a favorite restaurant in Edinburgh that I took the liberty of making a reservation at for the six of us. I'll send you the time and address. Attire is casual."

"Looking forward to seeing you again," Marie said and meant it. She found the German attractive both in looks, intelligence, and character.

"Tell Jo, I'm impressed with her suggestion, and I'll get right on it as you Americans like to say."

They ended their call, and Marie returned to the table with a broad smile on her face. She'd stepped into an alcove by the toilets to make the call.

"Henrik says he impressed with you Jo! He's also texting the restaurant address and time where he made reservations for tomorrow night for dinner. I'm glad we don't have to figure that out."

They finished dinner and discussed where to go next; there were comedy nightclubs, music, and whiskey bars under discussion.

"Why don't we do it all?" Angela suggested. "I thought the bar was pretty special back at the hotel. We could drink more whiskey and begin our search on Nick De Jong."

A short time later the group found themselves back at their hotel and in the Art Deco bar that had loads of atmosphere. They also had an excellent whiskey collection and the friends each ordered a new brand based on a discussion with the bartender.

"I love that the bartenders know the subtleties of these brands. It's part education part atmosphere to know a little of the story behind a certain distillery," Angela said sipping her brew. Then looking over at Nathan she added, "Sweetie you look like you could use two toothpicks to prop your eyelids open. You must be jet lagged; why don't you head upstairs to sleep. We're all on Scottish time and the night is young."

After a huge yawn, he stood up and said, "That's a brilliant idea. I think I'll do that."

"Babe if you can't fall asleep once you fall into bed, just come back down and rejoin us," Jill said before kissing Nathan as he left the bar.

Sipping their whiskeys, they doubled down trying to figure out who Nick was. Out of the side of her peripheral vision, Angela noticed one of their followers from earlier on the train. He passed through to the lobby desk.

"One of our four followers just arrived," Angela said in a soft voice. "He walked past the bar entrance toward the lobby desk. I'm going to slip out and see if I can get his picture."

"Well I've got your back," Marie said. "I'll just stay out of the way and make sure he doesn't try any funny stuff with you."

Jill watched them go thinking back to their first cases wherein she was the aggressive one, going the extra mile to collect information for their case. Now Angela or Marie would sometimes take a starring role, and she would marvel at their commitment and courage. Jo didn't lack courage or smarts, but she sometimes didn't pay attention and missed those opportunities that Marie and Angela took.

Marie was casually sipping her whiskey, leaning against the doorway, watching Angela work her magic. She checked her camera view then walked up to the man and tapped him on the back. As soon as he turned, she snapped a bunch of pictures, and said, "Oh sorry, I thought you were Andy Murray, the tennis star. So sorry," and she turned and walked away to the lobby restroom.

The man followed her retreat with a puzzled look on his face and then he turned and left the hotel lobby. Marie continued to lean, awaiting Angela's return from the bathroom. Perhaps it wasn't safe for them to visit locations alone with four unknown people on their trail. Marie wondered how he'd followed them to the hotel and where his male companion was – maybe they split up to look in different places.

Angela exited the restroom and returned to where Marie was standing and asked, "Is he gone?"

Marie nodded 'yes'.

"Awesome, I got some good pictures of his face. Let's find out who he is."

While Jill was running the picture through her database, Angela, Marie, and Jo were conferring on what they found on Nick.

A few minutes later Jill said the man's name was Girard LeRoux from France. "Let's see if he has any connection to Nick."

"Speaking of Nick, we've found that Nick was an only child, his parents are dead, divorced with no children and he owns the security company that we're aware of."

Angela was quiet and thinking, then she asked the other three, "Should we ask Henrik to bury him on his estate?" Then she winced and added, "I guess that would put Henrik on the spot."

"He'd be buried in Germany rather than his home country, but at least he'd be near a friend," Marie said. "Henrik's estate is so large that he won't even notice and at least someone will assume responsibility for his remains. It's not like we can take him back to Wisconsin; at least I don't know how he'd fit into our luggage allowance."

It was gallows humor, and they all laughed at that thought, then Jill added, "How about if Nathan suggests that to Henrik. It will be less pressure than coming from us."

"Brilliant idea, Jill, we'll do that," Angela agreed. "I guess we better focus on Girard LeRoux."

"Why don't you all focus on Nick and I'll see what I can find on Girard," Jill suggested.

According to what she read, Girard was working as a plumber in Rennes, France. So what was a plumber doing following them around? He was a few years older than Nick, so they could have met, except Nick seemed to have no connection to Rennes let alone France. She thought back to their conversations, but couldn't remember if he spoke French. Time to look for other commonalities in their background. Did he serve in the military? Was there anything linking him to Operation Gladio? How about his parents, was a father connected to Operation Gladio?

Using the techniques Marie had taught her, she searched a wide variety of social sites looking for more information, but she found next to nothing on the man. So far, she hadn't determined if he was even married. She gave in and said to the group, "I have a plumber from Rennes, France and not much more."

"No connection to Nick?" Jo asked.

"No, or to Operation Gladio," Jill sighed.

"Did you find him on social sites? How about the Plumber's Union of that town?" Marie suggested.

"Hmmm I'll try that," and the room went quiet again.

Ten minutes later Jill sighed and said, "Nothing. Marie do you want to take over this search?"

They changed assignments and silence reigned again.

A little later, they were all ready to give up. They had marginally more information on Nick and Girard, perhaps a little too much whiskey, and a little tiredness from the incident on the train.

Leaning back on her barstool Angela asked, "What's on our agenda tomorrow?"

"Let's go to the castle for starters," Jill replied.

"Haven't you had your castle fix yet?" Marie asked.

"No, I'll need at least another ten castles for my love of them to be satisfied."

"I need my beauty rest so how about planning on meeting at nine?" Jo replied. "Jill I assume you'll be up early because you always are and Nathan is still on the California time zone, and maybe Henrik will have something for you to sink your teeth into."

They said their goodnights and headed up the elevator to their rooms. Jill undressed, brushed her teeth and slipped into bed with Nathan. Curling into his warmth, she hoped that Henrik would indeed have new information for them by the morning.

$\mathcal{N}$athan was the first one awake the next day, being unable to sleep beyond five. When at home, he tried to avoid waking before eight and was grouchy until ten many mornings. This time he was the one wide awake at an obscene hour. He decided to wake up Jill and see if she was interested in starting the day with a little loving.

An hour and a half later they were walking into a café located in the hotel. Marie was already seated there with her computer and a large cup of coffee.

"Good morning!" Jill said. "How's your coffee?"

Marie, the coffee aficionado of the group, replied, "I read that in Scotland coffee is served in a bigger cup," and she held a larger coffee mug than they had seen in the UK, "and it's higher caffeine which suits me just fine. It's good."

"Have you had breakfast?" Nathan asked.

"No I figured you two would make your way down here first and I'd dine with you. Angela is still asleep, and we won't see Jo for a while."

A waitress came over to take their order, and they settled in with their own cups of coffee.

Jill looked through her emails, but there was nothing there yet from Henrik, and she said to Marie, "Too bad there's nothing here from Henrik. I guess I'm expecting too much from his super computer power."

"Actually, I received an email this morning from him, and I've been working on the information," Marie replied.

"Cool, anything of note so far?" Jill asked.

"Outside of his expected movement around Amsterdam and other cities where he controls hotel security, the other city he visited was Le Havre, France."

"Do you have a location specifically or a hotel he stayed at or did he even stay overnight?"

"Yes, no, and no," Marie replied with a smile. "I have a street filled with apartment buildings that he entered and exited with about a four-hour stay twice. He appeared to have not stayed in the city except for that meeting."

"Could he be providing security for such an apartment building?" Jill asked.

"Good question, I'll have to contact someone in his company and ask." Looking at her watch, she decided it was safe to call the company.

"Since it's been a few days since his death, I assume they know. They may not give us the information but I'm sure they know who we are after all of the dealings we've had with Nick and I think he had some of his staff guarding us in Amsterdam or Brussels," Jill mused.

A few minutes later they had their answer. They had no contracts for security in France and didn't manage any apartment buildings.

"So what do we do with that information?" Nathan asked.

Jill liked his use of the word 'we'. "We may not be able to do anything with that information. If this is a street with multiple apartment buildings, there could easily be one hundred addresses for us to check. Since we don't know the names of any other

Operation Gladio members, I'm not sure that we could identify where he visited."

"Even if you do know there's an apartment owned by one of its members, what does that tell you?"

Jill shrugged at Marie's question and replied, "Maybe it will be useful information later. I wonder if Henrik could use the symbol of the group and look for it on a person or something on that street. Nick's tattoo was barely visible, but maybe some of the other members don't have it tucked away like he did. It's worth a try."

Marie had been typing while Jill discussed the address issue. She liked the last idea and soon sent off an email to Henrik. It was great they had a responsive partner in this investigation like Henrik and his enormous capacity computer power.

Looking at the time, they realized that Angela and Jo would be joining them in about thirty minutes, so they ordered breakfast and planned the day ahead.

"Let's go to the castle first then explore the area around it. We'll grab lunch there, and perhaps Jo will have one of her walking tours of the area that are always fun to do. Henrik hasn't sent me an address yet, so I'm not sure how much time we'll need to travel to the restaurant, but I for one will want to change clothes since he's a more upscale kind of guy," Jill suggested.

After an impressive Scottish breakfast of porridge, bacon, and toast, they were joined by Jo and Angela and set out to walk to Edinburgh Castle. Besides the castle, there were gardens and the Portrait Gallery to view. It was the most visited site in Scotland and some parts of it dated back to 1200. Standing on top of one of the many walls of the castle looking out at the firth and farther on, the North Sea, the view was amazing.

Just a speck on the firth, almost where it met the North Sea was Inchkeith Island. Jill pointed to the island and said its name then added, "It's an interesting island from a medical viewpoint, during the last three or four hundred years people were sent there who were thought to be infectious. It seems that the Scots understood isolation techniques before the rest of the world. Then in WWII, it had a key military role for the UK watching out for submarines, and using spies to plan a fake attack on Norway. It's interesting to look at old war strategies that worked based on the lack of technology. Today we have satellites, and we would have easily seen the lack of troop build-up required to attack another country, but they didn't have that in the 1940s."

They were enjoying the views when Jill all of a sudden caught a movement out of the side of her eye. Someone was rushing at her, and so she ducked low instinctively. She had a range of thoughts shooting through her head. Maybe she hadn't seen the man. Maybe she looked like an idiot ducking imaginary creatures. Maybe her paranoid brain was making things up; she'd finally lost it. She felt something graze her shoulder which brought her back to reality and caused her to focus on the blur of motion.

A moment later she heard a yell as a man went sailing over the castle wall. They didn't hear a thunk below, but they could hear screams both male and female and crying coming from the castle grounds.

CHAPTER 16

They stood there shell-shocked over what had just happened.

"Oh my god, what was that?" Marie asked. "Or maybe I should say, who was that?"

"I caught motion out of the side of my eye; I saw a blur of motion toward me and instead of moving out of the way I ducked. I guess he, at least I think it was a he, had too much momentum and flew up and over me. I guess we better call the police. At least there were a lot of witnesses here to verify that we didn't throw him off," Jill said looking around at the gathering crowd wearing various degrees of shock on their faces.

A security person rushed over to them and asked everyone to stay where they were. Angela turned around and began taking panoramic photos of the crowd in case it was relevant later.

Jo said in a low voice, "I hope he didn't land on anyone below."

Nathan replied as the tallest of the group, "There was nothing below but wall and dirt, so unless someone was doing repairs, there wouldn't be anyone below." He'd been hugging Jill tight since the event. He had been studying the island that Jill was talking about when the blur of motion happened. He was so thankful that she had been paying attention. There would be no more tours of castle walls until the murderer was found he vowed. First Nick and now almost Jill. He just shuddered at the thought.

The security guard was keeping an eye on the crowd trying to hold everyone in place until the police arrived. Perhaps two minutes later he heard sirens approaching probably police, and an ambulance and in less than a minute two officers were walking across the grounds towards them. They briefly stopped, addressed the still stunned crowd, and said, "We are Police Scotland. Please stay where you are so that we may take your statements. This kind gentleman here is going to ask each of you for identification and contact information."

Handing a pad to the guard, they continued toward Jill and her group who were presently searching for their passports.

Holding out their badges for inspection the woman said, "I'm Sergeant Emily Robertson, and this is Constable Lewis Stewart. We'll also be joined eventually by the Major Investigative Team unit whenever they arrive. May I see some identification, please?"

The five of them stood holding out their passports. The Sergeant read all of them at a glance, while her Constable took down more detailed information.

"So you all are from the United States. Are you here on holiday?"

"Yes," Marie replied.

Looking at Jill, she asked, "Can you tell me what happened today? I understand a man went over the wall."

"Yes we were touring the castle and looking over that wall," Jill said pointing to where she'd been standing. "I was describing the history of Inchkeith Island when I noticed movement out of the corner of my eye as I turned to my right to talk to my friends. The man, at least I think it was a man, was moving fast at me, so I ducked, and that seemed to throw his momentum over the wall. I heard a wee bit of screaming after that although I'm not sure where it came from. My friend Angela, photographed the scene soon afterward so that you would have a record of who was around at the time."

The Sergeant squinted as if in pain, bracing for the explanation coming at her and asked, "Why would you think to do that?"

"To help the Police in their investigation," Angela answered.

"Are you law enforcement in the United States?" the Sergeant asked suspiciously.

"No," Jill answered. "I'm a forensic pathologist and a private investigator. These are my friends and part-time assistants when I get called in to consult on the cause of death."

"What do you think is the cause of death in this case?"

"I don't know where the man fell and I don't have any confirmation that he's dead. Is he?" Jill asked.

"We have a team searching below the wall, and they should confirm," and her explanation was cut off when her cell phone rang. She stepped away a moment to talk on the phone returning to the group. "Yes, I can confirm the man is dead."

"Then I would guess he died from massive brain trauma, or from a fracture of the cerebral spine," Jill said. "Sergeant, there may be an explanation for this man's behavior, and it may be connected to a death in Cardiff, Wales."

Jill could see two emotions warring with the Sergeant. Suspicion as to whether Jill was a nut case and dread that this was going to be a significant and exciting investigation that she would lose to the special team she mentioned. Looking over the Sergeant's shoulder, she could see another gentleman walking towards her in a plainclothes suit. He had red hair and the look of perpetually wind-blown cheeks. He was Nathan's height, fit, and Jill had to damp down a smile that came with imagining him in a kilt. Yes, this was likely the detective inspector.

Sure enough, Jill was right, "Hello, I'm Detective Inspector Jack Campbell. I'll just listen in on Sergeant Robertson's questions."

After the disruption, it took the Sergeant a moment to

remember the bombshell of Jill's statement and so she asked, "What do you mean tied to a murder in Cardiff?" There, that shocked the DI who had been oh so casual about joining the conversation. She saw him shift his weight out of the corner of her eye and pay attention to this woman that even she hadn't figured out yet.

As they talked, Jill had been searching her purse for the business cards of DIs Jones and Davies of Cardiff. She handed the cards to the two and waited for their reaction. She could tell that before she produced the cards, the conversation had gone poorly. The card captured the attention of these two Scottish police personnel, and she waited for the next question.

"Just a moment please," muttered DI Campbell, and he pulled the Sergeant away for a private conversation.

Jill turned her back on the two and said to her friends, "I'm sorry, but I think this is going to mess up our schedule today. I feel like I've jinxed our vacations now with murder always on the itinerary."

"Jill, we're just glad you're safe and remember we always have unique stories to tell about our vacations because of these adventures," Jo said. "Besides, culturally we're getting to know the Scots better."

Jill had to raise her eyebrows at that, "I don't know whether to laugh or cry at that statement."

DI Campbell and the Sergeant returned to their group and tried to enter the circle of friends, but they were doing a group hug ignoring the inspector for the moment.

"Ladies, I have more questions for you," came the stern but musical voice to Jill's ears.

They ended the hug quickly, and Jill said to the inspector, "Just a moment, please," mirroring his own words moments ago.

"Hey guys, I think I might have something here," Angela said holding out her camera.

"What did you and your camera discover?" Jill asked looking over at her friend.

She held the camera up to Jill and asked, "Is this man, the one you saw on the train that you thought was following us?"

Jill looked into the camera's screen and after studying the man agreed that he was one of the four they'd seen the previous day. She nodded and asked, "When did you take his picture?"

"Right after the man disappeared over the edge. I don't see him around now," Angela said looking around the castle battlements where they were standing.

The Detective Inspector was frustrated with being a few steps behind everyone else in this investigation. He reached for Angela's camera, and she was so surprised at his motion that she let go, letting the wrist strap slip off her arm.

"Ladies, my partner is calling the DIs from Cardiff to get your story. You apparently think that some man who has since disappeared had something to do with being a threat to you. If you'll send me that picture," he said to Angela while handing her his card, "I'll see if we can run the bloke down. Now I need to have my questions answered."

They nodded and waited patiently for him to begin. Jill gave him points for sorting through their conversation quickly.

"Usually I like to start at the beginning with a full explanation of, in this case, an attempted murder, but let's jump to the end. Why do you think some guy tried to murder you?"

Jill thought for a few seconds and then said, "We think he's related to a stay-behind army formed at the end of WWII to prevent the spread of communism. This theory will be confirmed when you do the autopsy and find a tattoo in this shape," she said finding the photo of Nick's tattoo on her phone.

Then she added, "Somehow the members of Operation Gladio have learned of our investigation into the death of our friend Nick Brouwer De Jong, and this is his tattoo that we found during his autopsy."

DI Campbell stood there a moment trying to decide if these Americans were nuts with such a far-out explanation. He'd never heard of stay behind armies or Operation Gladio which sounded Italian. He was jolted out of his mind sifting through a game plan, by a text from another member of the Major Investigative Team that verified the women's stories from the Cardiff inspectors.

They appeared to have a complex situation on their hands. It was neither a simple crime nor a short explanation. Campbell made a quick decision to have an MIT teammate interview the relevant witnesses and let the others go. He requested the security guard provide them with a private room for a discussion. Soon they found themselves in a back hallway that contained a small windowless conference room. The women, Nathan, and the DI sat down as he took out his notebook.

"Ms. Quint, may I see your identification again? Do you have a business card?"

"It's Dr. Quint as I'm a forensic pathologist, but you can call me Jill," she said as she showed him her PI license and business card.

"Who did you work for as a Pathologist?"

"The State of California Crime Lab."

"You're about as an informed witness as I've ever interviewed."

"I don't doubt that as in my former life as a State Employee, I never saw a crime committed or had one committed against me. Since I've become a consultant and my friends here provide assistance, we'd experienced multiple murder attempts against our person in Europe and the United States. So yes we're all informed witnesses based on our experiences over the last couple of years. That was why Angela was so quick to take a photo today; it's helped in the past."

"So at the Castle today, you were looking with your friends over the castle walls north and talking when you saw in your peripheral vision a man running at you. You ducked, and he went sailing over the castle wall? Did he hit any of your friends on the way over?"

"I felt something hit my head and by the time I looked up he wasn't in my line of vision," Angela said.

"How hard did he hit you? Do you have a bump? A headache?" Jill asked concerned and feeling guilty that she hadn't asked this question of her friends before.

"I'm fine! I think whatever it was, a hand a foot, or some other part of the body touched my hair enough to muss it up but not hurt my head," Angela replied.

"That's good," Campbell said. "The man dropped forty to fifty feet to the dirt below, not surviving the impact. He appears to be in his forties and has a French passport on him."

"Did the Cardiff inspectors tell you about the case there?" Jill asked.

"Yes, I believe a friend of yours was pushed off the tower at Cardiff Castle, and they've made little progress in solving the case so far including the real identity of your friend."

"Yes and I guess we better give them a call. We were able to identify him with the help of another friend in Germany. He's the CEO of a global security firm, and he really does have the best facial recognition software in the world. Despite hanging out with Nick off and on over two years, we never had a good photograph of him, and his face was damaged in the castle fall so we couldn't get one post-mortem."

"So the Cardiff police couldn't identify the murder victim?" Campbell asked in disbelief.

"All we could find up to the time of his murder was a history going back a few years; we could see the business he owned and operated but we're unable to find his birth, country of origin, or even family members. Since our friend found the information last night, we have all of that information," Marie replied.

"How about his fingerprints? Couldn't they have used them to identify him.?"

"Yes, but again the prints belonged to a man who arrived in the Netherlands a couple of years ago," Jill replied. "It was not the true identity of the victim."

"So now you have his full name, what else do you know?" Campbell asked.

"We tracked his movements across Europe over the past month," Jo said.

As this was the first time she spoke, Campbell paused assessing her comment and competence, and then he asked, "What did that tell you?"

"All of his movements made sense except a visit to Le Havre, France. We were debating what to do with that information when we decided to visit your castle. We think there could be up to one hundred different owners of property on that street and it's a case of us not recognizing good information when we have it," Marie said.

"What were you planning on doing next?" Campbell asked.

"Finish touring the castle, and then visit other sites around here like the portrait gallery," Angela said innocently.

"Sorry, I mean what were you going to do next on the case?" Campbell asked knowing the woman purposely misunderstood his question.

"We were going to research Girard LeRoux," Angela replied. She liked this DI, but she was also fed up with all of them lacking faith in their abilities to solve a crime.

"And who's that?" he asked with a hint of exaggerated patience.

"Might be the guy that just flew over the wall," Nathan offered, tiring of the conversation.

CHAPTER 17

"How do you know his name is Girard LeRoux," asked the detective his suspicions raised as he had not shared the identity of the man with the women. How could he be a stranger to them and yet they know his identity?

"He was one of four men that we think may have followed us on the train from Manchester to here yesterday. We tried some tricks in Glasgow, but he managed to follow us to our hotel last night and Angela took his picture," Jill replied.

DI Campbell wondered if he had fallen down the rabbit hole to the Mad-Hatters luncheon. He paused, contemplating which part of Jill's statement to ask about first.

He led with, "What tricks did you employ?"

"Two of us got off the train and went to the bus station with the help of Uber. The other two changed their appearance in the restroom and then took Uber to our hotel, but we were working in the hotel bar last evening when we saw him enter our lobby," Angela said and added, "I went up to him and tapped him on the shoulder and snapped his picture, then apologized for thinking he was Andy Murray."

Campbell couldn't help himself, and he let a laugh slip out at the ingenuity of this team, then a new thought came to him.

Looking at Nathan, he asked, "Where were you during all of these events?" He could think of a few sarcastic things to add but barely held on to his tongue.

"I was en route from California. I hadn't planned on joining their girl vacation until they reached Edinburgh. I reached the hotel about the same time they did last night and given the time difference between home and here I gave it up earlier than they did. Jill and I are staying a few extra days to explore some of your distilleries."

Dropping back to their question as to who was dead he said, "So you're correct about Mr. LeRoux. He's the one that went flying over the wall. He landed on his back, his face about the only thing undamaged. We identified him as we were walking into the conference room. How did you figure out who he was?" Campbell asked. Then he answered his own question, "Oh, you used that facial recognition software you mentioned that identified your friend."

"Yes," Marie replied.

"What else did you find on him?"

"I only had about twenty minutes last night before we went to bed, so I know he's a plumber from Rennes, France and has no obvious connection to Nick."

"Nick is your friend that was murdered in Cardiff," Campbell asked.

"Yes, or to Operation Gladio," Marie replied. "I'll be curious to see if he has a tattoo on him somewhere; that will tell us a lot."

"Tell me more about the tattoo," Campbell said.

"During his autopsy, we discovered a tattoo under Nick's hairline. It was small, and we had never seen it on him while he was alive," Jill said while showing the Inspector a copy of the seal. Nick's tattoo was too small to work out all of the detail when compared to the real seal that you could view in Wikipedia.

"I'll ask our pathologist to look for it. I believe you said there were four men following you on the train," Campbell prompted as he hadn't heard the rest of their story.

Jo interrupted him with "There were two groups following us. One was a set of two men, one who later appeared at the lobby desk and a short time ago went flying over the wall. The other pair was a couple, or at least they were trying to act like a couple, and we haven't seen them since Glasgow, or rather they haven't seen them as I don't notice people usually."

Again Campbell didn't know whether to laugh or sneer at her comment. These Americans were really keeping him unbalanced.

"Let me see the pictures you took of Mr. LeRoux, and of his friend," he asked Angela as she seemed to be the photographer of the group.

He said "Pardon me," and he tapped out a message to someone, then added, "I'm asking for help as there are a lot of moving parts in your stories."

"We don't have a photo of the couple, but Marie and Jill could probably describe them for a sketch artist if you have such a position in the Scottish police," Angela suggested.

DI Campbell spent a few moments mulling things over in his head. They didn't have such a position on their force, but he could use the resources of one out of Scotland Yard or MI6. He'd have one of the members of his team locate the service for him.

"I'll set that up," and he tapped out another text on his phone. "It likely won't happen today. How long are you planning to stay in Edinburgh and where are you going from here?" He asked as another thought occurred to him.

"We'll be here three days and then Marie, Jo and I are returning home. Jill and Nathan are staying a few additional days to visit distilleries," Angela replied.

"We're taking the train to St. Andrews tomorrow and might take in a round of golf. We might also visit the highlands the day after," Marie added.

"Playing the Old Course are ya?" Campbell asked a bit of a brogue coming through in his question.

"No, we can't meet the Handicap Maximum since none of us have one. We'll play Strathtyrum. We just don't take golf all that seriously," Jo replied.

"Yeah we talk while we swing, so you could send an artist out with us on the golf course, and he could easily develop a picture in between us taking shots," Angela replied.

"I'll keep that in mind," now he sounded like he was insulted at their lack of respect for the game.

"We've all won prizes for our golfing ability, and we like low scores as much as the next guy, but we see no reason to stress over it," Jill said.

Campbell looked at Nathan who just shrugged since he was used to their attitude. Then he decided to ruffle the detective's feathers and added, "Hey didn't you ladies have a murder at a hole at one golf course, then Angela here was shot by the murderer at another golf course evading him?"

"It was just a superficial wound that Jill treated and in the end, we solved that case."

"Does violence follow you ladies around?" Campbell asked.

"No, I would like to think it's more that we can mix vacation with a murder investigation and do both at the same time. Like we're doing on this trip. Think of all that we've contributed to the police investigation so far," Marie said.

"Would you mind sending me a picture of the man that disappeared after his friend went over the wall this morning," Campbell asked seeming all business after digressing for a short time over golf. "We'll want to identify him. Tell me more about this Operation Gladio. I've never heard of such an organization."

"We found it far-fetched ourselves when we stumbled across it. We're too young to understand the threat of communism, how people viewed the world at the end of WWII. It was something we studied in school as a way countries are categorized, but as Americans, we see communism as a failure in every country that it's been tried; Cuba, China, North Korea, and Laos and we're not worried about it taking over the world, but Europe has a different mindset. You all went to war twice at a great price and so this idea of a secret army to prevent communism perhaps makes more sense," Jill said.

"Did a stay-behind army do any good shortly after it was set up?" Campbell asked.

"They were rumored to have prevented left-wing takeovers in Greece and Spain. Our own CIA and your MI6 were rumored to be involved. I think this was before NATO was formed," Jo replied.

"So…" Campbell paused thinking through his question, "Why would your friend have been killed and what's their motive for hunting you down," he asked the group at large.

"We don't know," Marie shrugged. "Does anyone care if a stay-behind army exists at the moment? As for Nick since he had the tattoo, we think he was probably a member of the secret group given the secrecy of his background. Why else would his identity be so hard to find and his existence lacking details older than perhaps four years ago?"

"You say MI6 was involved? You're sure that the British version of your CIA had a role in Operation Gladio?"

"I think all the spy agencies of all western countries might have initially been involved with some sort of stay-behind army," Jo said.

"Did the Cardiff police follow up with MI6?"

"We don't know. I'm not sure they believed our research about Operation Gladio even with the presence of Nick's tattoo. I think they were relieved when we left Cardiff," Jill said.

Campbell sighed, but he'd pursued other very odd stories, and Edinburgh and its surrounding cities amounted to about one and a half million people which was sufficient to have created bizarre crime stories which is exactly where he would file this one. He thought he probably had the necessary information from the group and it was time to let them go.

Making sure each of them had his contact information and he theirs, he wrapped up the conversation. Walking them back to the public area of the castle, he thought of one more question, "Dr. Quint, do you have a desire to be at the autopsy of the man that tried to kill you?"

"Only if your staff fails to find the tattoo that matches what our friend Nick had. I think it'll be a fairly obvious cause of death finding."

Watching the detective stride away, Angela asked, "So where to now?"

CHAPTER 18

"I'd say a pub where we can all toast Jill surviving another murder attempt, but I don't have a desire for alcohol at the moment," Jo said. "I suppose we could try some tea."

They all looked to Jill for her decision as it had been her near-death experience. She stood loosely in Nathan's embrace, his hands on her shoulders staring at the wall over which Girard had traveled.

"If I could find a cupcake shop, then a ridiculously sweet cupcake would do the trick of cleansing my palate of this morning's events."

Her grinning friends all quickly looked around for Jill's heart desire of the moment. Two blocks off of Princes Street, they found a café that served cupcakes and tea. Her friends weren't nearly as fond of the concoctions as she was, but fortunately, there were a few other items on the bakery's menu.

"Nothing like a blast of sugar to lighten one's mood," Jill said. "I'm ready to resume being a tourist! Should we head to the Portrait Gallery now?"

"We're close to our hotel," Angela noted. "We could stop there and use the facilities, and do a quick search on our suspect, then leave for the Gallery."

"I second that idea," Marie said. "Jill, don't you want to brush the sugar off of your teeth?"

"Despite my love of cupcakes, my teeth haven't fallen out yet, but we can satisfy everyone's curiosity since we're close."

Less than five minutes later, Jill had set the facial recognition program to search the picture of the accomplice. Then she headed to her bathroom to brush her teeth, use the toilet and wash her hands. She applied minor repairs to her make-up and re-entered the living space where everyone was gathered around her laptop watching the database think and search.

"You know guys the database doesn't work faster because you stare at it. We could go back out and come back later to results," Jill said as the computer screen paused and then came up with a match. "I guess I shortened the search time by selecting Europe as the home of this guy rather than worldwide."

Looking at the screen, all five of them gathered around to see the result. It was a man by the name of Giovanni Floris from the Italian island of Sardinia.

"We should probably share this with DI Campbell," Jo suggested.

"Interesting that Nick was from the Netherlands, Girard from France, and now this guy from Italy," Marie mused. "Perhaps there's like one man from each country left in the group." Pausing she added, "They didn't let women into this group right?"

"Right, no women in Operation Gladio or indeed in anything I read about stay-behind armies," Angela agreed, "But perhaps they belonged in secret."

"What's your next step, now that you've identified a potential co-conspirator?" Nathan asked. "Are you going to stay here and research him?"

"Sweetie, you've hung around us enough to guess our next move," Jill said. "Soon you'll be on the payroll too."

"No thanks, I don't want to get entangled in your investigations. I'm just here to cover your six," Nathan said with a smile.

"Let's pass the name on to our Detective Inspector and see how far he gets with researching the man. Maybe he'll be as good as us, and we won't have to give up our vacation time to run down this group," Jill suggested.

"The last few cases have shown us to be usually a few steps ahead of the cops, so it's likely we would do a better job," Marie said with a bit of a protest.

"I think we need someone to take this Operation Gladio seriously," Angela replied. "I don't think we were convinced that Cardiff took us serious enough to call MI6 and have them research the group. So maybe Campbell will be more invested in the case if he does the research."

"I don't know that a few hours are going to make a difference, so we'll give him a few hours head start and see what happens," Jill suggested looking at her friends for agreement.

She dropped an email to the detective then they all set off back towards Princes Street and the Scottish National Gallery. They visited all three galleries and their gift shops thanks to a shuttle bus that circled between the three locations, then moved on to the gardens. As it was fall, the leaves were changing, and the gardens were a little barer than they'd be at the height of the summer, but they were still beautiful. Sadly they had a view of the castle wall where the unfortunate Mr. LeRoux went flying over and could imagine the fall to his death. They quickly walked away from that view.

Angela and Jill had visited the city before but had not had the opportunity to walk up to Arthur's Seat. It had been on their to-do list when planning this visit. Jill wanted to see it for its vistas - she loved standing atop mountains gazing at the horizon while Angela knew she'd get some great photographs from the highest point in the city. Taking Uber to the closest walking path, they quickly scrambled to the top of the mountain and spent half an hour enjoying the view; while Jill breathed in deeply several times seemingly cleansing herself of the day's angst. When they all had their fill of the location, they returned to town and their hotel to get ready to dine with Henrik.

Nathan had agreed to approach him in private concerning the burial site for Nick. In fact, they were sending him ahead of the women so that Nick could ask him that question as well as discuss an evaluation of a winery that Henrik was thinking of purchasing in the Rhine region of Germany. The ladies would follow about twenty minutes later that way Henrik would have the undiluted attention of Nathan while he discussed the business opportunity with an expert like Nathan. They all knew that once the women joined them the topic of conversation would be Nick's murder.

Henrik had chosen a restaurant that seated ten customers in a small dining room within a four block walk of their hotel. He was heading home to Germany after they ate. As soon as the ladies had given him a date, he called and booked the restaurant. Despite the fact they had just six customers another four were not added. Their conversation of friendship was occasionally broken up by the two brothers that served as cooks, sommeliers, and wait staff. The brothers had to think it was the oddest conversation they ever eavesdropped on as they were talking about a murder with American and German accents. Even Jill who avoided unusual food or spices enjoyed her meal with the proclamation that she didn't want to know what it was that she was eating.

"Did you hear back from your detective about the presence of Giovanni Floris?" Henrik asked.

"Not yet so my bet is they haven't been able to identify him on their own systems. In the end, I think you'll have another customer Henrik."

"I should just pay you guys to fly around the world and solve crimes in my sales division. You could have the fun of solving crimes, and I'll get sales. What do you think?"

"Much as we love you as a friend Henrik, we don't want to work for you. We like taking jobs on at our leisure," Jill replied.

"You mean taking a job every time you come to Europe?" he said shrewdly.

"Hey, there weren't any murders when we visited you at your house last time!" Marie said.

"That's probably because you went directly to my home from the airport," Henrik said.

From there they went on to a discussion of Operation Gladio. As a German, Henrik had another opinion of stay behind armies. While he was too young to remember the moods of his country after WWII, he did remember earlier years when there was shame for having unleashed Hitler on the world. Even today America had formal military bases in Germany, so what would be the point of a secret stay-behind army if you already have the real thing?

"Did you ask your own Federal Bureau of Investigation if they knew if you had a stay-behind army?" Henrik asked familiar with U.S. law enforcement agencies as customers of his company.

"I did, and they said no such thing existed, end of story," Jill said. "I didn't ask the CIA, and I'm not sure they would give me an honest answer even if I did ask."

"Now it appears that you have photographed three men that belong to Operation Gladio, two dead and one still alive. Correct?" Henrik asked.

"Correct," Angela said.

"You have Nick on the street in Le Havre; I could run a check on the other two, Girard and Giovanni and see if they are sighted on the same street and maybe then look at who else is on the street around the same time. The result of that search might expand your list of people that belong to the Operation. Really what you want to do is capture one of them and see what is going on - does the group exist and was one of them a murderer of Nick?"

"Exactly!" exclaimed Marie.

"Maybe I could have the Cardiff police check Nick's extremities for fingerprints from Girard," Jill said. "We'd then have confirmation of his killer; not that it makes any difference at this point as Nick and he are both dead, but it would close the case for Cardiff."

She pulled out her phone and texted that question to DIs Jones and Davies.

"So you have this group of people that are the remnants of a bigger operation from the 1950s and 1960s, and because they haven't done anything in decades, no one cares about their existence. Right?" Henrik asked.

The four women nodded their heads in agreement.

"You ladies care because you want to find Nick's killer and someone is making attempts on your lives. With this Operation Gladio, you don't know if there is one remaining member or twenty that will continue to pursue you."

"Jeez Henrik, I was upset with the one killer. Why did you have to mention twenty?" Jill lamented.

He smiled and continued, "You also had this couple following you that are apparently easy to shake as you haven't seen them since the train station in Glasgow. Your Edinburgh Police are not going to care about your plight if Girard is proven as the killer of Nick, correct?"

"Except we have this guy still running around named Giovanni Floris that might be trying to kill us, or perhaps he gave up and went home to Sardinia," Angela suggested.

"If you've kept a covert operation secret for two decades, is that the kind of person to give up and go home before their perceived mission is finished?"

"You know Henrik, I'm going to need a few more whiskeys if you keep up with these stark tones," Nathan said. "It's real depressing listening to you and knowing that you're probably right."

Sending a pained look at Nathan, he relented and said, "Perhaps I am wrong about these men and their motives."

"No, I think you're probably right," Jo agreed. "We'd better watch our backs. Being pushed to my death is not my chosen method of dying, and that appears to be their modus operandi."

Jo's comment really said something. If she was feeling the threat of this group, then it had to be obvious and evident and not a function of Jill's overactive imagination.

"Henrik, you bring up a point on the couple. Were they following us or were they following Giovanni and Girard? Perhaps the reason we haven't seen them is that they're not following us," Marie speculated. "I didn't notice that couple around us in the time immediately after Girard went over the castle's wall, but it was so shocking that I'm not sure I could tell if we had bright sun or cloudy skies at that time."

"I left my camera memory card back in the hotel room, but let's look at it when we get back to see if the couple is there in the background anywhere," Angela said. "I never saw them in person so I wouldn't have noticed them in the background. Isn't it strange that the Operation Gladio guys knew where to find us in Edinburgh?"

"Unless Nick mentioned his itinerary..." Marie suggested.

"Maybe," Angela said thoughtfully as the group lapsed into a temporary silence.

Nathan broke the silence with, "Hey Henrik has agreed to host Nick into perpetuity. We were discussing funeral arrangements, and we thought we would hold a service in about two weeks, Henrik has generously offered to fly us in for the event. So we would have the memorial on a Saturday and fly back to the US on Sunday. He's also sending a few buses to Nick's company so they can join us in celebrating his life."

They were relieved that the guys had worked out what to do with Nick's remains.

"Thank you, Henrik," Angela said on a somber note. "Do you need any help planning the ceremony? Do you have a pastor that will officiate? I know that Nick wasn't a devout Christian, but he was one none the less, and his soul should leave this world to Corinthians or Ecclesiastes."

"Angela, I'm afraid that it's not my area of expertise, would you mind arranging for a pastor?" Henrik suggested. "I would look for a service in English as that is likely the common language among his employees, and us."

Angela nodded her acceptance of the assignment, then added, "In America, we have a meal after a funeral and feed the mourners. Perhaps we could do more like an Irish wake with lots of beer and stories about Nick. I'm sure his employees have stories we haven't heard, and it would be nice to share."

Henrik announced he'd take care of the details and invited everyone to send him an email with their requests. Setting a time for the service, they ended their discussion about Nick and the plans to get the friends back to Germany to celebrate Nick's passing.

Henrik had a two-hour flight back to Stuttgart, and it was getting late. He hated to cut the night short as he always enjoyed talking to the Americans. They had a different view of the world that he enjoyed and understanding how they went about their investigations gave him ideas for potential innovations in his software. Their next gathering would be sad, but he knew them well enough to know there would be a party atmosphere to send Nick off to the next world. After that, he was meeting them in New Orleans where they were all invited panelists to a national gathering of private investigators. Jill's team were doing a panel presentation and spending a few days enjoying the city. Henrik's was launching a subscription service for his technology for small users like private investigators and had an exhibit booth and a panel presentation, but he'd make time to relax with them. Jill had solved the murder of his wife Laura and often when he dined with the Americans, he felt her presence nearby as though she had a seat at their table. Weird.

CHAPTER 19

They walked back to their hotel enjoying the opportunity to walk off the fabulous dinner they'd just had. The streets were quiet as the area was more residential than bars and restaurants.

"Is Henrik going to buy the vineyard he discussed with you?" Jill asked.

"I think so. Of course, it all depends on a final price for land and business, but it had many strong qualities about it. Their wines were excellent, but their marketing and branding was horrible. I had suggestions on how he could improve both with my help."

"Are you going to seek a part ownership with him?" Jill asked. Nathan was looking for investments in the wine industry as it was something he understood from a business perspective.

"No. I don't feel comfortable investing outside of the United States. The rules are so different for property and business decision making that I don't feel like a partner. If Henrik gets the vineyard, I'll fix the branding and marketing. We might have a few more trips to his estate while I work on it."

"If he sends his private plane and we can make that stop in

Wisconsin, we could all have a couple of four day weekends in Germany," Jill suggested.

"That's the plan, I told him rather than hiring me, I'll do it for free if it involved trips on his jet. He agreed, and we'll sign a no-cost contract if it comes to that. So keep your fingers crossed."

"Is the vineyard near his estate?" Marie asked.

"Yes, it's in Württemberg, which is a wine growing region that includes Stuttgart. It's mostly farms and hills and so lends itself to vineyards. It's also in the more southern area, so it has a longer growing season."

"Sounds exciting. I'd offer Henrik free financial services, but I'm sure he has a string of accountants to advise him," Jo suggested.

"I think he'd appreciate your offer and the next time you see him face to face you can make it," Nathan said. "He values your friendship and wisdom."

"If you're doing the marketing and branding perhaps I can do the photographs that you'll need," Angela offered.

"That sounds like a plan to me, but you'll have to travel to Germany when I go despite whatever schedule you have in Wisconsin. I'll be on a tight timeline, but I can give you the dates now, and you can let me know if you're available."

Angela was thinking of her upcoming schedule, and she had no weddings planned, and she could move anything else around a few days to accommodate Nathan's needs.

"I can work under those restrictions, send me any sketches or thoughts you have for the materials that way I can think about capturing those images," Angela replied.

"I feel like I'm constantly the paranoid person of this group, but there's a couple that have been following us from the restaurant about a block behind us," Jill said in a soft voice. "How about we turn as one and head back to the restaurant to pick up something we left behind - how about a favorite scarf? Angela, can you get a picture of the couple?"

Nathan hesitated wondering about Jill's instinct to head into confrontation rather than away from it, but then he shrugged and thought better to confront than get stabbed in the back.

Marie said, "If it's the couple from the train, they looked harmless."

Angela nodded her agreement on the photo and Jo nodded her agreement.

Jill said out loud in case the couple was within hearing distance, "Oh rats! I forgot my scarf at the restaurant. Let's head back there since it's my favorite."

The group turned around and headed back to the restaurant startling the couple walking toward them. Angela was zooming in her focus to get the couple's faces, snapping pictures. Jill saw them hesitate and quickly confer as to next steps; aiming their faces down, as they continued walking toward the group.

Still in a loud voice, as they approached the couple, Jill looked up and smiling ruefully said, "I can't believe I left that scarf behind. Oh well, I needed to walk off dinner."

Marie, taking a leaf out of Jill's playbook looked at the couple and said, "Do I know you from somewhere? Perhaps we met in Sofia when I was there for my nephew's track race?"

The female shook her head and said, "No we haven't met."

Jill tried to detect where the woman's English accent was from but failed.

Angela added, "I like your outfit. I'm taking your picture so I can remember what to buy to get your look," snapping photos of the couple as she spoke.

The couple just walked around the group and hurried on their way as Jill and her group continued on their path for another two blocks. Not observing the couple since they walked away they turned around and headed back to their hotel.

Jill said laughing, "Angela, anyone that knows you was laughing their head off when you said you liked her outfit and were taking a picture to remember what to buy. As if!"

"I know my ribs are hurting from not laughing and my nose is still tingling from holding back the snorts," Jo said talking and laughing at the same time.

"Why do you think I ended up coughing in front of them," Marie said. "It was either that or laugh. You know we'd make bad covert people since we can barely control our laughter when one of us acts out of character."

"Go ahead and make fun of me, but it was all I could think of at the time."

"You ladies are being hard on Angela," Nathan said while putting his hand on her shoulder in a measure of support. "Who will have the last laugh if she has a perfect photo of those two. Let's look at your pictures Angela."

They gathered around Angela as she looked at the screen of her camera toggling through her recent pictures. She had several good headshots of the couple for them to use later in identification.

"Great pictures Angela, but I still say your comment about the outfit was funny. In fact, it would have been funny if any of us had said it as it's so not us as a group to care about that," Jo said.

"Yeah, I guess I felt silly when I said it, but it was the first thing that popped into my mind. Since we've arrived back at the hotel, shall we all meet in the bar in say ten minutes?"

With nods of agreement, they rode the elevator to their floors and soon found themselves settled in the bar. After a debate about mixing whiskey with the wine from their meal, they decided to risk their heads, and each made a whiskey selection.

Jill uploaded the couple's pictures from Angela's camera, and they all got a look at them on a bigger screen.

"You got several good pictures, Angela!" Jill said. "What about their accents? Any guess as to where they're from?"

"The four words the woman said were not enough for me to guess," Nathan said, and there were nods from the others in agreement. "I would have guessed German, but I get that mixed up with Danish and Dutch."

"I agree with Nathan that it sounded Germanic, but it could have been one of those other languages, or maybe Swedish or Norwegian," Angela said. "I think we are so far from knowing that it's pointless to guess."

"Okay, let's search for faces and try to figure out what this couple has in common with Operation Gladio," Jill said. "I suppose they could have been just your average pickpocket thieves, but why would they follow us on the train here and why go after a group as large as us? It's easier to mug a lone person. So I think they have to be connected to the Operation."

She'd been typing as she talked and soon they were watching the hourglass spin as the computer went to work matching the pictures. Knowing it would take some time they worked on their plan for the next day.

"We could rent a car and explore the distilleries around here," Angela suggested. "Or maybe check out the train schedule since we wouldn't need a designated driver. We would see more of the countryside of Scotland which I would love to do."

"If we had time to travel, I would say let's go to the Island of Islay," Marie said. "I'm a Scottish landowner there, and I'd love to visit my square foot of land."

"Really! You never told me you owned land there!" Angela said.

"Would we all fit on your square foot?" Jo asked.

"Let's check the plane schedule maybe we could fly?" Nathan said. "Where exactly is this island?"

"I checked it out before we left and it's about 200 miles away as the bird flies, but it's a seven-hour drive through the countryside. I didn't check the air routes."

Nathan had been researching the island while they talked and said, "We could book roundtrip air for under two hundred dollars leaving Glasgow at 8:30 and arrive in Islay at 9:15 and leave at five pm. Your distillery, Marie is about six miles away, and it looks like we could hit four or five there. Shall I book us flights?"

The group looked at each other then smiled and held their whiskeys up for a toast, while Jo said, "Nathan, book our flights!"

"Imagine how safe we'll be there!' Angela said. "It's too remote for them, and if they aren't on our flight, then they will have to charter a plane to catch up."

Nathan added, "They have bike tours, but I think we lack the time to do that, so I'll rent a car for us."

"What else can you do on the Island," Marie asked.

"If you were into birds, it's paradise. There's a golf course and an American Monument to a ship sunk in World War I. I don't think we have the time to do that. I think we should plan on touring the four distilleries, eat lunch at one of their stops, and explore the two cities of Bowman and Port Ellen."

"You make a great tour guide," Jo said. "That's plenty of action, and we'll have to find a way to Glasgow in the early morning and back in the evening."

"We also have to stand on Marie's land," Jill said. "Do you know how to find it?"

"Yes, they sent me a Google Earth view of the foot, and their website says they'll provide a jacket and wellingtons so I can reach my land."

"What an adventure!" Jo lifted her glass again and said, "To Nathan for providing us a well-timed escape in the middle of another interesting vacation."

Then they heard Jill's computer beep that the search was finished and they turned and gathered around the screen.

CHAPTER 20

The couple walked away from the five Americans saying little. Once they were two blocks away and assured they couldn't be heard by anyone, they spoke in a language other than English.

"In my years of doing recovery work, that was the strangest interaction with someone I've been following," the man said.

"I wonder why they wanted our picture since I'm sure they got it?" the woman questioned.

"Normally I would say they took the picture so they could identify us, but they're tourists; how would they have access to any databases that have our information in them?"

"True, but the one woman is listed as a private investigator in the United States, so she probably knows something about how to identify us."

"Yes, but our cover is solid, so even if she identifies us German citizens, she won't have much more than that since we're school-teachers from Berlin."

"Didn't you say that one of the group was a photographer? Was she the one that took our picture? What do we know about the man in that group?"

"He just appeared in Edinburgh and judging from his body language, he's connected to the woman that's the private investigator," the man said.

"Let's identify him when we get back to our hotel. I wonder how they know Nick? They seem so American."

"Nick said he was meeting some friends in Wales and we just assumed they were Dutch friends, but maybe it was these Americans. Certainly, someone brought them into this situation. I wish we hadn't missed those first few hours after his death; then this whole situation might make more sense."

"He suspected that someone from his group was following him; he was fearful that there were agents unhappy with dissolving the group of which he was the most vocal supporter of dissolution."

"What do we want from these Americans?" the man asked. "Do we think that Nick passed on information to them before his death?"

"I don't know; after all, we don't even know what stolen item he came across. All we know was he wanted to meet us shortly after someone shoved him out a castle window, and it was expected to be a short meeting - he said ten minutes."

CHAPTER 21

"Hmmm," Jill said.

Angela read aloud, "Michael Schmidt and Nicole Becker, country of residence, Germany. Occupation on their passports is listed as school teachers. Why would two German teachers follow four Americans or a Frenchman or Italian from Operation Gladio?"

"That's the twenty-five thousand dollar question," remarked Marie.

"We'll have to review our materials on Operation Gladio. I don't remember any German influence," Jo said.

"Me either," Marie said.

"Ladies, I'm still jet-lagged," Nathan said standing up. "I'm going to go upstairs and finish arrangements for tomorrow and hit the sack. I'll send you a text for our departure time from this hotel in the morning, and you can set your alarms accordingly."

They went back to exploring a connection between Germany and Operation Gladio. They received a message from Nathan that he rented a car for tomorrow and based on the internet they should plan on leaving the hotel at 6:30 in the morning.

"I hate 6:30 departures on vacation, but I'm not surprised since the plane leaves at 8:30. At least we don't have to go through immigration and customs on this short flight."

An hour later, Marie landed on a site that hinted that one of the duties of a stay-behind army like Operation Gladio was the successful search for loot that the Nazi's stole from the citizens of the countries they invaded.

"I wonder if they had any success in locating stolen property?" Jo asked after Marie explained the connection she'd just found. "Maybe any recovered loot went to finance their continued operation as it's not clear where their funding came from in recent times."

"I don't know, this article is the only one that has made reference to a connection to the hunt for Nazi stolen goods, maybe it's a rumor," Marie acknowledged.

"If only Nick was alive to tell us," Jo lamented.

"Think back to our conversation with him, did he ever sound like he was hunting for or had found a treasure?" Jill Said.

There was silence as they contemplated their conversations with their deceased friend. Jo shook her head first, then Marie followed with, "I don't ever recall him saying anything about searching for gold or being a detective."

"Me, either," acknowledged Jill.

"Perhaps Nick discovered some connection to the rumored gold location," Angela said.

"But why would people be after us?" Jill asked. "Does someone think he shared that information with us or passed it to us in code, or there was something on his person at the time of his death or during his autopsy that would have pointed us to that fact?"

"Maybe we should ask the police in Cardiff for a copy of the contents in his pockets or his cellphone," Marie suggested.

"The police wouldn't give us his personal effects as we have no legal right to them," Jill said.

"What if we tell the police that we're taking responsibility for his funeral as they and we have been unable to locate any living relatives; do you think they would turn over the contents to us along with his remains?" Angela asked.

"Perhaps, since I assume they matched Nick's killer to the man in the custody of Edinburgh's police," Jill speculated. "Let me give it a try. I'll email the detector inspectors now with our plans for Nick's remains and see if we can get those personal effects. I'll have to coordinate with Henrik as I would assume he'll have to make arrangements for the pick-up and storage of Nick until we return in a few weeks on his jet to Germany for a proper funeral. I could walk Henrik's representative through the personal contents and get the stuff delivered to us by the time we return from Islay Island tomorrow. We only have another two days together to solve this case. Nathan and I are staying on two days beyond your departure, but I don't think the answers lie in Scotland; they're likely back at wherever Operation Gladio's headquarters are."

"Sounds like a plan, I'll work on getting Henrik's representative moving on this now, Jill you handle the communication with the Welsh detectives and then we sleep on it overnight, have fun in Islay in the morning and hopefully have new material delivered to us tomorrow," Marie said.

CHAPTER 22

The next morning they were in the boarding area of the Glasgow airport waiting to board their plane. Henrik's representative was in Cardiff and by the time they landed at Islay, he expected to have the personal effects of Nick, and they would go over them via video conference so that he would know what to have delivered to Jill and company later that day. She briefly debated just having him send everything, but she'd have a hard time believing he would have something secret sewn into his underwear. Certainly, they wanted all of Nick's electronic possessions. Perhaps the hospital or pathologist routinely disposed of clothing cut off someone after their death; they would wait and see.

Jill, Angela, Nathan, and Marie were on the outlook for someone following them to the airport and on to the boarding gate, but so far they hadn't seen anyone suspicious including the German couple from the previous night. Once they got to the island, it would be hard to hide in the limited population there.

After landing on the island, they looked around again at the people and found no one to be concerned with and were soon in a rental car heading for the first of five distilleries. Nathan was their designated driver; he planned to taste and then spit all whiskey samples, that way he could explore the flavors without being impacted by the alcohol content. They also would have a big lunch in Bowman, the largest city on the island. Anyone following them would have to charter a plane to land after them, and by then they'd hopefully be at their first distillery miles from the airport. They went first to the distillery where Marie owned her one square foot plot of land. As it was still early in the morning to be drinking whiskey, they got directions on where to hike to find her plot.

It was rough going in patches with uneven ground, moist boggy soil, and a few limestone rocks were thrown in for good measure. The view was spectacular with a craggy coast, and they tried to see both Ireland, about twenty-five miles away, and another Scottish island about the same distance. Winds were known to blow up to one-hundred and fifteen miles per hour in the winter, but fortunately, it was only blowing a mild wind as they stood close to the coast. The wind played havoc with their hair, so they quickly admired the view before taking various poses around Marie's plot of land before heading back. Once back at the distillery, the five of them looked into all of them acquiring their square foot of land adjacent to each other. They'd feel much more like landowners if they shared a total of five square feet. Finally, they started their tour viewing a warehouse with aging oak casks of whiskey.

Their tour guide used a corkscrew type of device to remove the cork from the barrel. He then used a metal thing that looked like a syringe from a 1920s Norman Rockwell painting to remove a sample of the spirit. He poured the sample into a glass and Jill was amazed at how similar this experience was to that of a winery as they reviewed the sample for clarity, aroma, and taste. He pronounced that the whiskey was ready for bottling. Nathan and Jill peppered the guide with questions given that this was a sister industry to their own of operating a winery or doing the wine labels and marketing pieces like Nathan did.

From this distillery, they moved on to the town of Port Ellen where they had a fantastic meal at a local hotel. They ordered two soups - a harvest festival consisting of soup made from local vegetables and Cullen skink, sort of a fish stew, but more flavorful than American chowder. They chose a variety of main courses like fish and chips where the Haddock was sourced from local fisherman. Their desserts were diverse ranging from a lemon tart to Jill's favorite Crème Brûlée, and Jo's favorite, Sticky Toffee Pudding.

"Between that huge lunch and the whiskey, I could take a nap now," Jo said and then added with a grin. "We could inquire as to whether they rent rooms by the hour."

"With that question, we would live up to our reputations as Americans. I'm not sure reception would believe we're not planning a fivesome!" Jill said wrinkling her nose.

"I second that," said Marie stifling a yawn.

"I'm ready to move on to additional distilleries," Angela said. "I'm so glad that we agreed to spend the day visiting Marie's land. I love this island, and I've enjoyed visiting the smaller distilleries here. I mean they're small in comparison to say Glen Livet or Dewar's. It's rather like visiting a Wisconsin winery in comparison to Napa Valley. They make great wine, but the weather limits the types of grapes. Here I think it's just the remoteness of the island."

"I'm with Angela," Nathan said. "I love visiting these distilleries. Ladies, forget the hourly bed rental and let's get going, the slugs can stay in the car at the next distillery and take a nap."

It was rare that Nathan pushed them to anywhere, but visiting the distilleries had given him a charge like he'd imbibed large mugs of coffee rather than small shot glasses of whiskey. The four women just gave him an indulgent smile and followed him to their car.

Four distilleries later, they each had a set or more of whiskey glasses and whatever other stuff they'd bought at each gift shop. By the third distillery, they'd taken to Nathan's practice of spitting out, rather than swallowing the whiskey. It was the only way to stay sober enough to employ their senses discovering the subtle flavors of the spirit.

As they were closing upon the dinner hour, they found themselves back at the Islay island airport ready to head back to Glasgow where they planned to grab dinner before returning to Edinburgh. Nathan smiled as Marie and Jo drifted into sleep immediately after take-off. Jill and Angela were never able to sleep on a plane as both were too uncomfortable; one too tall and the other too short for the headrest.

Hours later they found themselves back at the hotel where a package awaited them from Cardiff. Henrik's assistant had collected the belongings including his clothing that he wore at the time of his fall. They all agreed to let the assistant meticulously examine the clothing for hidden pockets or writings or anything unusual on the clothing that could turn into a clue. They knew the Cardiff crime scene staff had already performed such a search and so they expected nothing. Apparently, the final search had yielded nothing, so the package contained a cell phone, wallet, car keys, gum, and a few loose pieces of paper. Nick's body was on its way to a mortuary near Henrik's home, and they would have a memorial service for him the following month when they returned for the long weekend to help Henrik with his newly acquired vineyard.

Jill had looked through the envelope at the reception desk with the others standing around her. She glanced up and asked, "Should we go to the bar and examine these items or one of our rooms?"

"Our rooms are small, and we've had sufficient privacy and internet access in the bar," Angela replied. "Besides after that dinner, I might have another whiskey! You know, when in Scotland, try lots of whiskeys."

"I don't think we'll be looked upon well here if we taste then spit out the whiskey," Marie said.

"I'll just have bottled water," Jo said. "I have probably met my whiskey quota for the year today. While I can distinguish the subtle flavors of the spirit, I prefer beer or wine."

"I agree with you there, and that's why I grow grapes and not hops in my fields."

"Let's meet down at the bar in say fifteen minutes?" Angela suggested.

"I think I'll pass on your meeting," Nathan said. "I'm not sure I can help, and I need to sketch out some ideas from what I saw today."

Marie replied, "Sounds like a plan and we'll call you if we need you."

They took the elevator up to their floor and entered each of their rooms. They unpacked their purchases, hung up coats and other cold-weather gear, performed their ablutions, grabbed their purses and various computers and took the elevator down to the lobby.

They walked into the bar, and Angela froze with her friends bumping into her from behind. She stepped back, and they gave her space with a whispered 'what!' from one of them as they ducked behind the doorway.

CHAPTER 23

Angela whispered, "Our couple from last night is already in the bar. I don't think they saw me enter and back out. What should we do?"

"Is the bar busy?" Jo asked.

"Yes, relatively so," Angela replied.

"Then let's go in and sit down at the opposite end of the bar and wait for them to come to us," Jo replied. "We'll be safe as there's a crowd of people around and no tall building or castle wall to toss us off of."

As no one had a better idea than that, they proceeded into the bar and spread out at a table. A waitress came over and took their drink order - a whiskey and three glasses of water, and she departed. The women continued to discuss Nick's possessions that were sent to them. They turned on his phone which was getting low on the battery but fortunately Jo's phone had the appropriate cable to power it, but it was pass coded. They hadn't a clue on the password especially since his keyboard was in Dutch with different letters where the E,R,S,C, and M keys were on an English keyboard.

"Let me translate the words, perhaps it also has a finger code on it, and I recall his fingers being relatively okay from the autopsy," Jill said.

There was silence in the bar, and she looked up to see various expressions of revulsion on her friends' faces.

"What? Do we want to solve a mystery here or what!"

When her friends' expressions still hadn't changed, she said, "Look I give you guys permission before I get cremated to use my fingers to unlock my phone for any photos you might want from it."

With that Jo burst out laughing, "Only a pathologist could think that way, but personally, I have no intention of doing that. If I didn't get any photos I wanted from you in your lifetime, then it wasn't meant for me to have a copy."

Marie added, "Jill we'll let you do the honors with the phone and Nick's fingers. I'd rather contact Henrik and see if he can suggest a less morbid way to handle this phone."

"That's a good idea, Marie," Jill said. "I should have thought of that."

Just as Marie left her barstool, to make the call to Henrik, her exit was blocked by the approaching couple.

"Hello, we would like to ask you questions," said Nicole Becker.

She found four American women staring back at her unwilling to commit to providing her with answers, just waiting patiently for the questions.

Jill raised her eyebrows as if to say 'go ahead'.

There was a quick rapid fire conversation between Nicole and Michael in what Jill assumed was German before the first question was produced.

Again there was a rapid-fire conversation in German, then she said, "May we join you?"

Jill had been putting away Nick's possessions into the padded envelope they were mailed in when Michael had first spoken, now she said hesitantly, "Sure, and will you tell us why two German school teachers are following us?"

The pair borrowed chairs from other tables and gathered around with Jill's team.

Ignoring Jill's question, Michael instead asked, "How well did you know Nick Brouwer?"

When the four women stared at him in silence unwilling to give any information to these complete strangers, he added, "We were working with Nick at the time of his death. He mentioned he was meeting some friends in Wales, but we assumed those friends were Dutch or maybe Belgian not American. Were you friends of Nick?"

"What were you working with Nick on?" Jo asked.

Good question Jill thought. They were dancing around something with this couple, but neither wanted to show their cards yet. Again there was another rapid-fire conversation in German.

"You know, you just make the four of us suspicious when you switch to another language for a conversation. It's human nature you know," Angela said.

"We work for Brisdale's. Have you heard of this company?" Michael asked while nodding his head at Angela acknowledging her comment.

"Yes, you're an auction house based in London perhaps with locations around the world," Marie said as her friends nodded.

"Usually we verify the provenance of pieces that owners wish to sell through the auction house. We also spend about a quarter of our time searching for as yet to be recovered paintings, gold, jewelry, and sculptures from WWI and WWII. Nick had some information about the location of a fairly large example of Nazi stolen goods. We wanted to know if he shared that information with you?" Nicole said.

There was silence around the table as the women again thought back to their conversations with Nick and then Jill spoke up, "We asked ourselves earlier if Nick ever gave us any indication that he was searching for some hidden treasure including the infamous Nazi gold train and the answer was no."

"What do you mean a large example of Nazi stolen goods?" Angela asked. "Is that based on the quantity or quality of a particular item or is that reference to the physical size?"

Michael Schmidt sighed then said, "Nick was involved in a group that he couldn't tell us about other than to say he thought it was about to dissolve and he thought one or two of the members were about to close in on a big collection of stolen goods from World War II and he somehow had the impression that the group members wouldn't be handing it over to the rightful members."

The women looked at each other debating whether to say something, then Jill said, "Would you mind stepping away from our table? We need to have a private discussion and to verify your story. Give us twenty minutes."

Nicole Becker looked as though she wanted to argue with them, but Michael grabbed her elbow and pulled her away saying over his shoulder, "Come get us when you're ready to talk."

Marie had gone to work the moment they said they were employed by the auction house proving the provenance of artworks. Why had their other search identified them as school teachers?

Around her, Jill, Angela, and Jo were discussing their impressions of the couple. After following several more threads, she looked up and said, "Here's their story. Their passport application clearly hasn't been updated to reflect their current jobs which I did verify from other sources. Their degrees are in fine art, and they taught at the High School level. Their Master's thesis was about the effects of war on stolen art. Five years after becoming teachers, they changed jobs and went to work at Brisdale's."

"Are they married?" asked Angela.

"I don't believe so, let me check," Marie replied.

A few clicks later, she said, "No, just co-workers."

"Is there a downside to letting them into our investigation?" Jo asked.

"Only if they're not who they say they are and are instead related to Girard LeRoux. Then they might be after something we know or an item among Nick's possessions," Jill replied.

"If that were the case, why not just kill or kidnap us until we hand over the goods?" Angela said. "I think they had the opportunity to do that over the past couple of days. Marie, do you see anything in their profile that would lead us to think they were dangerous? Or if you put your HR hat on, is there anything there that would stop you from hiring them?"

"Good questions, Angela, let me think."

Her other three friends sat there looking at her waiting for her to come to a conclusion. She was very good at detecting lies and judging people; far better than her three friends. She thought back to what she'd read about this couple and decided, in the end, there wasn't anything suspicious about them.

"I would hire them. I think we can trust them."

Jill looked up as Nathan entered the bar walking toward their table. She'd sent him a text when they first sat down after noticing the couple advising him to finish whatever he was doing. She knew from experience that when he was in the creative zone, it was best to leave him there unless there was an emergency. She'd assured him they were perfectly safe and to join them if and when he felt like it.

"What's going on? Have they made a move toward you guys?"

"Yeah, they came over and asked us if we were friends of Nick," Angela said

"Really? I bet you had such choice words about that question. What are you doing now?"

"We researched them again, this time a little more in depth," Marie replied. "We just decided that we would welcome a conversation with them since they asked us some questions about Nick."

"This could be an interesting night," he noted and got nods of agreement from the four women.

Angela stood up and said, "Should I go get them now or do we have anything more to discuss amongst ourselves?"

"We'll just wing the conversation," Jo said. "I'm getting tired of the games we have to play with your spies and otherwise bad people. We're safe here in this public bar, so nothing too terrible can happen."

Jill filed away Jo's concern for the future trying to avoid using her services on the general parts of the case and instead direct her to accounting questions. There, Jo was in her element searching for evidence of fraudulent accounting practices, and the tension of a new case didn't seem to reach her through the zone she was in while studying numbers and balance sheets.

Angela nodded agreement to her friends' head nods and verbal comments and stood up to retrieve the couple.

CHAPTER 24

Giovanni Floris was sitting in a tiny hotel room in Scotland. He felt like his world had been heaved up in the air by a dog with big teeth that soon proceeded to shake him. Operation Gladio had voted to dissolve, a shocking occurrence to him. He didn't want it to end. He'd been involved for fifteen years after he completed his military service in Italy and his father had served before him. He liked his fellow members and appreciated they were from all over Europe. When Girard had voted against dissolving the group, he'd thrown his vote with him as he thought others would raise their hands, but he was wrong. Now he wasn't sure what to do next or whether the police were looking for him. Thinking back to his actions, he wasn't in the United Kingdom when Girard killed Nick Brouwer, but while he had an idea that Girard was going to kill that woman, he'd done nothing.

He wasn't a leader; instead, he'd always followed someone else in Operation Gladio or had been directed by Jean-Louis. With Girard dead should he return to his real job in Sardinia? Consider the Operation at an end? Find the women and kill them, then go home? He knew he could not turn around and kill his fellow order members even if they no longer wanted to be a stay-behind army. He was at a loss.

What was the treasure that Girard hinted at knowing? He planned to give the details of what he knew the evening before his death, but he'd been so busy trying to tail the four women that Girard never had the chance to resume that conversation. Had any other members known about this hidden treasure? Had Nick been killed because he wanted to end the Operation or over an argument about the treasure?

He could stay in Scotland a few more days and watch the Americans. Surely, they would go home soon. He thought Girard was following them because he believed that Nick Brouwer told them something about the treasure. It was why Girard lost his mind and attempted to push the woman over the castle wall. Maybe he should stay close so he could hear what they were saying. Then again if they knew where the treasure was, why were they in Scotland? Were they searching for it in Edinburgh?

He knew that over the years the Operation had found and secretly returned some spoils of war and when they couldn't find the rightful owner, they'd sold the items to pay for their ongoing operation. NATO had stopped their funding thirty years ago, and they had kept going on minimal funds from two countries that still supported the stay-behind army. Their financing was deeply buried as a military expenditure, and it paid for the upkeep of their apartment in Le Havre and ammunition since they all practiced shooting. As none of them were receiving a salary for their work for the Operation, they all had day jobs which significantly reduced their effectiveness as an Operation.

Then Giovanni got a bright idea. Would Jean-Louis reactivate Operation Gladio if he could find the potential treasure that Girard mentioned? If the treasure was worth a lot of money, then he bet Jean-Louis and the others would vote to keep the Operation going. They enjoyed each other's company and staying prepared for covert action. Maybe he could re-invigorate the whole group with enough money. So he needed to think about his conversation with Girard and where he knew him and possibly Nick to have traveled over the last several months. He would also concentrate on a word for word replay of what exactly Girard said. He was due back at his own job in a few days. If he couldn't figure out what the treasure was and its location, he'd have to work on it later when he had time off work.

Giovanni sat with pen and paper and tried to recall every conversation he had with Girard over the past week. An hour later, he had two full sheets of notes. He reviewed them and compared them to a calendar in his head and considered whether he documented every conversation. When he thought he'd got them all, he reread his notes and thought about clues in Girard's words. There was something there that he couldn't put together related to the Nazis. What was it?

Like other Italian schoolchildren, he had learned about World War II in his history classes. He didn't remember any discussion about the Nazis looting people and cities, but wasn't that always a part of war? He thought about the concentration camps he remembered learning about were related to Hitler and the Jewish people. Sardinia had lost its Jewish population to concentration camps elsewhere in Europe, but his history lessons were primarily about Mussolini. So he began searching the internet to refresh his memory about the war.

Whose treasure was it? Something hidden by a Jewish family before they were sent to a camp or perhaps something of the Germans or maybe Hitler in particular? Girard was from France and Nick was from the Netherlands, and both of those countries fell to the Germans in WWII, but for some reason, he ruled both countries out as well as his native Italy. He didn't think the treasure was in his native Italy as the flow of the war would probably preclude that region. He felt that Girard's mention of Northern Europe was likely the hiding place, but he was scratching his head trying to remember if he said Northern Europe or the Northern UK.

What was the treasure? Was it art or money or gold? Was he looking for something small like jewelry, something medium-sized like art or something substantial like stacks of cash and or gold? He was a simple plumber, not someone up on the politics of a war that ended nearly eighty years ago. Giovanni went to work on investigating treasures from the war. He hoped he was right about it being WWII, but again it was the only war that he associated with concentration camps. Had Girard said concentration camps or just camp like he attended as a kid?

He also thought about the word quarry, or was it quail? The words were similar sounding in Guernésiais. He was aware of the marble mined in Carrara in the northern tip of Italy, but he was back to there being no concentration camps in that area, but there were kid camps everywhere, so that didn't limit his search. In fact, he looked for concentration camps specifically in Italy, and none were near the famous marble quarry. Giovanni thought he would waste a lot of time looking at concentration camps as they were all over Europe at one point in the war. There were quail all over Europe and here in Scotland. Instead, he looked for the northern-most cities that the Germans occupied as they would have had to conquer a city before setting up a concentration camp. Was northern Europe Germany or Poland? Or was it Lithuania, Latvia, and Estonia? He would have to study more cities of Europe to answer his own question and what if it was the northern UK? Where had the Germans been in Scotland or had they been anywhere in this region? Did the actual battlefield extend this far west?

CHAPTER 25

*A*ngela approached the couple and invited them back to their table. The friends waited while the two Germans settled at their table.

"Ask away," Jill said forgetting where they had ended their conversation with the two Germans.

"Did Nick ever mention a hidden treasure, or otherwise comment on art or gold?" Nicole asked.

"No, he never seemed like he was searching for something. How did you meet him?" Angela asked.

"I met him perhaps two or three years ago at an auction in Amsterdam. He was providing security, and the story of stolen artwork was an issue raised during the auction. We spent some time talking about it," Michael replied.

"So how did you run into him again and what exactly did he say about a treasure?" Jill asked. She was puzzled over this entire situation.

"We ran into Nick about a few weeks ago by chance at the Stuttgart train station. He appeared to have a lot on his mind and asked us some questions about our work. In particular, he seemed to have questions about where we found stolen art or other arti-facts that came into the possession of Brisdale's."

"So he wanted a further explanation of how he went about establishing provenance for a particular piece that an owner wants you to auction?" Marie asked.

"No, it was more a discussion of what cities contained stolen Nazi art. The largest cache of goods was found in Austria in a city called Altaussee which was about fifty miles from one of Hitler's homes in Germany, but that was shortly after the war's end. Nick was more interested in what other cities contained hidden Nazi valuables. He asked about what we had found in Poland or one of the former Russian states of Latvia or Lithuania, or Scotland."

"Was there any Nazi treasure in those countries?" Nathan asked.

"Poland, yes. As recently as two years ago, treasure hunters were convinced they'd found secret tunnels in a city called Walbrzych. After millions were spent digging, the tunnel was declared to be the result of ice formations and no real discoveries have been made in that country. As for the former Russian states, valuables taken from Jews before their death in the concentration camps were melted down, and gold and gemstones outside of their original settings are nearly impossible to trace."

"Has most of the stolen Nazi stuff been discovered by now?" Jo asked.

"Actually, there are famous Renoir and Matisse paintings miss-ing. In total it's estimated that there are still one hundred thou-sand works of art missing," Nicole replied. "We don't know if some of the art was destroyed by the Nazis, by the war, or whether it's hidden by some collector who may or may not know its provenance."

"Wow," exclaimed Jo and Jill in unison.

Angela had been listening to the discussion and injected an idea into the group, "We have Nick's personal stuff, and maybe if we look through it, we might find information that will lead to the trail Nick was following."

"You have his possessions, why?" Michael asked. "Shouldn't they have gone to his family?"

"Turns out we were his family," Angela said with a catch in her voice as Jo and Nathan each reached over to rub her shoulders. "His parents are dead, he has no siblings, never married nor had any children. A friend of ours is burying him on his land in Germany, outside of Stuttgart."

"Oh," Nicole said and then assessing Angela's response added, "I'm sorry for your loss."

"May I see his phone?" Michael asked.

"No," replied Angela. "It's one of the few possessions we have and besides the phone is locked."

"I know someone that might be able to unlock it for you," Nicole offered.

"That's okay, we have our own expert who will get it unlocked for us," Jill said. "We really can't let it go out of our sight. I trust the expert that I will have trying to unlock the phone, you, on the other hand, might accidentally damage it."

"Okay," Nicole said sensing that she wasn't going to move these people on the issue of the cellphone. "When will you have it opened?"

"Tonight or tomorrow. We had dinner with a friend who's a security expert, and he's sending me someone to access the phone," Jill said.

"Tomorrow is also our last day in Scotland as we return home the following day," Marie said. "Jill and Nathan are staying a few more days. So you may have to follow us home to the United States to get access to any of Nick's belongings."

"Or you could wait perhaps four to six weeks from now when we'll have a memorial service for Nick near Stuttgart," Angela offered.

"We're anxious to have answers as soon as possible, and so if need be, we'll follow you to the United States," Michael replied.

With Michael's response, Jill and friends understood the depth of this couple's passion for finding the truth about further Nazi seized property, or perhaps it's what Brisdale's expected of its employees.

"Why don't we trade contact information and then we'll get in touch with you as soon as we have something," Jill suggested.

The couple offered this information as did Jill and soon they left the bar.

After they exited Nathan asked, "So what do you think?"

The women looked blankly at him not sure which aspect of the situation referred to his question.

"I mean do you think they're legitimate?"

"Yeah," said Angela and Marie. Jill nodded, and Jo shrugged.

"What an interesting case! Imagine how famous you'll be if there's something on Nick's phone that points you to the Nazi gold or art. I like this mystery better than your murder investigation," Nathan said.

"This is a murder investigation first and a treasure hunt second," Jill replied.

"Yes but you solved the murder. It was the man that tried to push you over the wall."

"Yes, you're correct that we know who killed Nick, but we don't know why. If we don't know that then how do we know if this case is at an end?" Jill reasoned. "We were suspicious at one time of a second man being involved in this whole thing, but we haven't circled back to that. If there's a second man, there may be a third, and we may be dealing with an organization."

"That's a lot of maybes, but I understand your caution. So what are your next steps?"

"I already contacted Henrik, and he's able to send his phone expert here tonight," Marie said. "I was working out the arrangements once I knew our direction. Henrik found a room for him in this hotel, and he'll be here in about two hours."

"That's past my bedtime," Jill said. "Nathan, you're the night owl amongst us, will you meet him and deal with him?"

"Sure babe."

"So tomorrow we're going to Aberdeen or did we decide on Glasgow?" Jo asked.

"We couldn't make up our minds so we'll flip a coin. Heads for Aberdeen, tails for Glasgow," Angela said.

"I think we should go to Glasgow, I checked the train schedule and it takes three hours to reach Aberdeen and Glasgow is a bigger city with more stuff to see and do," Nathan said.

"Ever our travel planner," Jo said. "I agree with Nathan, let's take the shorter train ride. I'll visit Aberdeen on my next trip to Scotland."

"Okay, Mr. Travel Planner do you have a time we should depart?" Marie asked.

"The trains go by every fifteen minutes so we can leave when people want to."

They worked out a time to meet the next morning, and all adjourned to their rooms. Nathan decided to wait for Henrik's man in the hotel bar. He could get some work done and not disturb Jill. They made sure the phone was the only electronic item in Nick's possession at the time of his death, and it was. He took his laptop and Nick's phone to await the arrival of Henrik's person.

Nathan had been deep in the design work of a new glass for a friend that he'd made beer glasses for. Seeing the shot glasses in the distilleries had given him an idea for a beer glass. He felt someone touch his arm and he looked up into the eyes of a young woman.

"Are you Herr Conroy?" the woman asked.

"Yes. Do you work for Henrik Klein?"

"Yes, I'm Anna. I understand you have a phone that you need to access. May I see it?"

Nathan wondered if the woman was old enough to drink, but

he supposed that was where tech skills were to be found these days.

"Would you like something to drink? That is if you're old enough to drink."

She laughed and said, "Herr Conroy, I'm twenty-two, so I'm old enough to drink, but I don't want alcohol to cloud my brain so I would like a decaf coffee if they have it, if not then tea."

Nathan ordered two decafs and came back to the table with them. The woman unloaded a few items from her shoulder bag. One device scanned the phone, but Nathan wasn't sure exactly what the device was doing. Instead, he said, "Do you think you'll crack it in the next hour?"

She looked up and smiled, "Nineteen minutes."

Wow, he decided not to interrupt her anymore and went back to playing with his glass design. He jumped when he heard her say, "Done."

She handed the phone to him and said, "I reset the passcode to my uncle's last name which is five-five-three-four-six that way it is still locked but none of you will forget the passcode."

"Thanks! Who's your uncle?"

"Henrik Klein. Klein is five-five-three-four-six on your keypad."

"Wow, so those computer brains run in the family?"

"Uncle Henrik has ten nieces and nephews, but only two of us are hackers."

"No wonder you arrived so fast here, he must have sent you on his plane."

"Yes, and tomorrow I'm going to explore this city for a day as payment for doing him a favor before I head back to work at home. Here's my card if you need me tomorrow for anything."

When Nathan returned to their room, Jill woke up. She was a light sleeper, and though he'd tried over their years together to avoid waking her up, it was nearly impossible.

He heard her voice in the dark ask, "Is he going to have the phone unlocked before we leave Scotland?"

"She already unlocked the phone," Nathan said, and Jill could hear the grin in his voice. She reached over and turned the bedside lamp on. While squinting against the sudden light, she put her hand out and said, "Give it to me."

He did and waited for her to ask the next question.

"What's the unlock code?"

"Klein"

"Huh?

"Five-five-three-four-six. It's how you spell Klein on a keyboard," and then Nathan took pity on her as he watched her active brain try to get into gear after being woken up from a dead sleep. "The tech was Henrik's niece, and she thought if she used his last name for the passcode, we would remember it. She also gave me her card if you have any problems tomorrow."

"Tomorrow! I'm going to review what's on this phone now and see if there are any clues."

Nathan just shook his head and changed out of his street clothes. He lifted the sheets to get into bed beside Jill who was sitting upright against the bed's headboard.

"Damn! I bet there's a thousand pictures, hundreds of text messages and emails written in a variety of languages. We'll need a translator to get through this stuff," Jill said scanning through the email messages.

"You can forward the emails to your computer and use Google Translate to read the messages for you no matter if they're written in German, Dutch or French. You're an early riser. Why don't you fall asleep now and get up at your usual time and peruse the phone."

"I'm excited about this new information. I don't think I can fall asleep."

"Perhaps we should use this bed to do something else besides sleeping or viewing a phone," Nathan said, demonstrating what was on his mind.

CHAPTER 26

As Nathan predicted, Jill was up early. After quietly dressing for the day, she left the room, Nick's cell phone and her computer in hand. The bar doubled as a coffee bar in the morning, so she settled there planning on getting work done while waiting for her friends and Nathan to appear. She knew he'd set his alarm as they wouldn't otherwise see him before ten and they planned to be in Glasgow by then.

She began by viewing the recent pictures. Nick had taken a few during the weekend at Henrik's a month or so ago, and that gave her a chronological starting place. She smiled at a few of the pictures taken of her friends; there were some great pictures of Angela. Since Angela was so often their photographer on vacation, there were fewer pictures of her than the rest of them generally in their vacation photo collections.

There were other pictures too including the typical shots taken of your feet when you don't realize the camera function is on. There were also some landscape shots. A couple Jill thought she recognized from Belgium, but she wasn't sure of the other locations. Were they random pictures or had Nick been photographing a potential Nazi gold train location? She thought that if she'd looked at the pictures a month ago, she might have wondered where they were taken, but thought nothing more of the location.

What could she do with random landscape locations? She looked up as Marie approached the table.

"Good morning. What did you find on Nick's phone?" Marie asked recognizing the phone in her hand as Nick's.

"Some good pictures of Angela and some landscapes I don't recognize."

"Can you use Henrik's software to identify the location? Any sign of the Germans this morning?"

Jill hit her forehead and said, "Duh, why didn't I think of that? Haven't seen them yet. Maybe I should text them to ride the train with us this morning so they can view the pictures."

"Let me see the pictures of Angela." After viewing several, she added, "Yep those are keepers. They're some of the best I've ever seen of her."

"How do I send these to my computer? My email isn't on Nick's phone."

"Could you text them to your phone then use your phone to email them to yourself?"

"Sounds like a plan. There's probably a faster way, but I don't know what it is."

"I guess you should text the Germans and have them meet us at the train station," Marie added.

Soon they were joined by Angela, then Jo, and finally as it was getting close to the time to leave for the train station, Nathan arrived.

As they were exiting the hotel, the German couple was already outside waiting at the curb. "We thought we'd walk with you to the train station," Nicole said. "What did you find on the phone?"

"Pretty much what any of us have on our phones – pictures, emails, and texts. Unfortunately, none of us speak a second language so we can't read the Dutch or German – or whatever language it's written in."

"I speak both of those languages and could translate for you," Michael offered.

"That's okay. I'm going to use Google translate. It's slower but safer. No offense, but I still don't trust you, so there's a limit to our sharing with you. We have landscapes we hope to identify with software, but if you recognize any of the locations, it will go faster. It's too hard to show you stuff on the phone and walk, so let's just sit close on the train," Jill suggested.

She watched as the couple searched for another solution and thought of none. The walk to the train station was short, fifteen minutes, then a little more time passed as they purchased tickets and found the track for their train. Fortunately, the train was waiting on the platform, and they could board immediately. It was apparent this was a commuter train as many people were dressed in business attire. They couldn't find seven seats together and ended up pairing off in twos. Nicole asked Nathan's permission to sit next to Jill, and he agreed as he'd planned to fall back asleep.

As soon as everyone settled in their seats, Jill and Nicole went to work on the phone, while Jo and Angela planned their itinerary for their Glasgow sightseeing excursion. Marie and Michael spoke of his travels as someone connected to the art world. He was very well-traveled, and it was fascinating to get his view as a European on the various countries of the world. Marie walked away with some notes for future vacation choices.

Jill and Nicole meanwhile were going through Nick's phone. Nicole glanced at the email titles, and they sorted through hundreds of emails including some from Jill and Angela. There were one or two emails in a language that Nicole didn't know. They tried Google Translate, and the language wasn't recognized.

"Maybe this is French, but it's written in code?" Nicole offered. "It looks a little like French, but it's not."

"We need to find some language expert to review it to verify that it's not an obscure language versus something written in code. I bet there are a variety of languages that are spoken by a small number of people. Certainly, in Google Translate, I don't see any Native American languages like Cherokee or say, Oneida. I bet there are perhaps hundreds of languages that aren't in this software so let's find a website that is more inclusive."

After a quick search, they found online resources to help, but their train was pulling into the Glasgow station. They were out of time for the moment.

"Will you forward one of the emails to me so I can figure it out while you folks are sightseeing?"

"Sure," and Jill did so. "How about I forward a few of the landscape pictures to you as well. We'll text you when we're ready to return tonight, and we can catch up then."

Jill could tell that Nicole wasn't satisfied with the plan, but she also knew no persuasion would work to get Jill to give her Nick's phone. With that Jill turned off all thoughts about the mystery of Nick and instead focused on having a splendid day in Glasgow on the last day of her vacation with her friends.

Jo and Angela directed their day visiting the highlights of Glasgow – the Kelvingrove Art Gallery, the People's Palace, and the Botanic Gardens. Along the way, they sampled food and visited merchant stalls buying small items to take home with them. All too soon they returned to the train station for the ride back to Edinburgh notifying Nicole and Michael of their travel arrangements.

Jill was excited to see what Nicole had found in her absence. Were the strange words a language her software hadn't recognized, or a code? If it was a code, how would she go about understanding it?

Soon they were all aboard another commuter train back to Edinburgh, and while it was busy, they all found seats although not in the same rail car.

Jo remarked, "It would be a long ride home if you had to stand for over an hour."

"Perhaps you can't do that on one of these railcars; they may cap ticket sales by the number of seats," Angela suggested.

"Yes, you're probably right about that," Jill said. "Europe and the UK figured out trains far sooner than the United States."

"They probably have fairly accurate projections of ridership," Jo said. "They have a lot of experience, and they can probably add railcars for peak times."

"Spoken like a true accountant," Nathan said with a smile.

"Just saying that's how I would manage the system," Jo smiled back.

Soon they were settled in their seats and Jill and Nicole huddled together on Nick's phone.

"What have you found out?" Jill asked.

"I contacted a language professor at Humboldt-Universität zu Berlin," Nicole replied.

"I assume that's a University in Berlin?" Jill asked thinking that Humboldt was a northern coastal region back in her home state of California.

"Yes, I checked, and it has the best reputation for languages. We were lucky in that the professor had a few students at his disposal and they love questions like mine. In about three hours they called me back with the information that the language was Guernésiais, a rare language from the island of Guernsey. My professor said that something like between one-thousand and two thousand persons speak the language."

"Wow, Nick spoke many languages Dutch, French, German, English and now this Guernésiais."

"Yes, he was good with languages. I have software on my laptop now to translate each email."

"Do you think we should focus on the emails in that language?" Jill asked.

"Yes. There was no reason for Nick Brouwer to speak that language," Nicole said simply.

Jill thought about her statement for a moment and agreed. Nick wasn't from that region and to the best of her knowledge had no business there, and it was a very rare language. With that conclusion, she began forwarding a series of about twenty emails in total to Nicole. The two stared at each email as the translation software revealed it.

A few emails were reminders of meeting times sent by an unknown sender; unknown as far as the sender's name meant nothing. It was titled, 'Server". As it was a proper name, the software didn't translate it, but Jill and Nicole understood the word.

One email was from Girard LeRoux, the man that had pushed Nick out the window, including that last meeting time at the Cardiff Castle. Nick hadn't had time to delete it. She noted that contrary to what he told them about arriving by train, he instead arrived by plane. She supposed that made sense when you looked at the transit time on the train from the Netherlands to Wales; he would have been unable to reach them on just a morning train ride. Perhaps she misunderstood his travel details. Or perhaps he couldn't keep the facts straight between his real and secret lives.

Jill tuned back into Nicole's translation process to see if anything more came to light.

Looking through the multiple translations, she asked, "Is that all of the emails I sent you?"

Nicole nodded a 'yes'.

"Let me see if there are any messages in his trash in that language," Jill said. However when she looked his trash was empty. "He must have had his phone set to empty the trash frequently as it's empty. Darn."

Nicole looked deflated by the finding. They hadn't found any useful information in regards to the Nazi loot yet.

"Let's move on to the pictures. I may be able to use some software to identify the location of a picture. Let's give it a try," Jill said, but then she felt the train braking and heard the announcement that they were arriving at their destination.

She looked at Nicole and said, "This is the last night my friends and I are together, and we're going to enjoy ourselves and perhaps celebrate Nick's life. They leave early in the morning, and Nathan will be a while waking up so you and I can meet as early as seven in the morning in the hotel bar."

Nicole looked disappointed but knew she wouldn't move Jill to share anything. With a sigh, she prepared to exit the train with all the other passengers knowing she'd have another crack at the phone's information the next day.

Angela led the group that night with help from Nathan visiting a variety of pubs to try a variety of beers. They'd all had plenty of whiskeys thus far on the trip and were at their core beer and wine drinkers. They ordered up dinner at one pub known for its food and had dessert in another pub before dragging themselves off to bed just after midnight.

Jill got up early the next morning to see her three friends off to the airport. They knew they were getting together in a month or so for Nick's funeral in Germany, but the end of vacations was always sad.

She was seated in the hotel bar eating breakfast and sipping coffee when Nicole and Michael walked in.

CHAPTER 27

*J*ill looked up as she said, "Hey there."

Michael offered to take care of breakfast for all of them, but Jill indicated that she'd already dined, but wouldn't mind an additional cup of coffee.

As Michael took care of that, Nicole asked, "Did you have a nice evening with your friends?"

Jill marveled at the sense of formality and manners that would allow the woman to delay her own gratification by asking if Jill had found something rather than the usual niceties of ordering breakfast and inquiring about her friends. Jill thought if the situation were reversed she'd likely not be so gracious. It was a lesson for the future that sometimes it was more important to waste seconds of time to share your humanity with the world.

"We had a fabulous time in the pubs last night, and I saw them off in their airport shuttle about an hour ago," Jill said looking at her watch. "How about you and Michael, did you have a chance to explore this town?"

"We ate at a nice German restaurant that featured excellent sauerkraut and beer. We spent some time studying the significance of the Guernésiais language, trying to understand why your friend would have communicated with it."

"It is a puzzle. I wonder if Nick's ever visited the Island of Guernsey? Certainly, if he never did, that would suggest the rare language was the language of his organization - the stay-behind army. What did you come up with?"

Nicole looked momentarily puzzled, so Jill added, "Did you and Michael learn anything new in your focus on the language?"

Jill knew she needed to focus speaking in full sentences rather than her own, at times, colloquial English.

Nicole smiled with an understanding of Jill's question and replied, "After researching the language in depth, we came to the same conclusion as you did - it must be the organization that speaks the language. The language has been around for one thousand years, but the German occupation of the island during World War II nearly eliminated the language. The Islanders had advance warning of the coming army, and many evacuated to other parts of the UK, and the language started to die out as after the war many didn't return to the island. Guernsey is trying to revitalize it by requiring it be taught in school, but most fluent speakers are over the age of fifty which Nick was not. So I think additional research into the language won't get us to know if Nick Brouwer was successful at locating the Nazi Gold train or some other stolen artifacts."

"How about if I work on the emails and you and Michael work on the pictures on his cell phone? It's all we have left to pursue. I asked a computer expert about using facial recognition software to identify the location of the pictures. He suggested that instead, I use a program that Google created that can look at a picture and identify the continent and country. I'll forward you the link for that, then start sending you the pictures from the camera."

Jill looked to Nicole and Michael, who had returned to the table, to get their feedback on her suggestion. After looking at each other and shrugging, Michael said, "I don't have any better ideas at this time."

The three of them got to work chasing words and pictures. An hour later Nathan appeared in the bar. He had a meeting with a potential new client at a relatively new distillery. They were picking him up in thirty minutes, and Jill had opted to stay in Edinburgh when he first arranged the meeting. Now instead of shopping or playing tourist, she would work with her new German acquaintances to see if they could identify the possible source of the hypothetical treasure.

Jill took a break from their research and sat with Nathan while he ate breakfast and worked on erasing the last vestiges of sleep. He wanted the account from the distillery. He already had many customers from the wine industry and then two from the craft beer industry, but today's meeting would be the new industry of spirits and whisky in particular. It might open new avenues of creativity for him. By the time he finished breakfast, his ride had arrived.

He leaned down to kiss Jill murmuring, "Stay safe inside the pub. I'll see you this evening with a dinner recommendation in hand from the distillery. Love you."

Jill raised her brows at his request that she stay inside the pub all day, but merely murmured back at him, "Love you too, and good luck with this potential client."

They parted, and Jill returned to her seat and laptop continuing the translations. After another hour of work, Jill checked in with Nicole and Michael.

"Have you guys found anything yet?"

"This software is great. We recognized a few of the pictures on Nick's phone and the software got it right also. At the moment, we entered into Poland according to the software. We looked up the locations that Nick's company says it manages the security for on his website and he had none in Poland. So I guess that's a positive sign; there's not an immediately logical reason for him to have been in Poland."

Their laptop made a sound and then Michael added, "And now we have entered Lithuania."

"Is that significant?" Jill asked.

"Significant?" Nicole asked.

"What role did Lithuania have with stolen Nazi loot?" Jill asked.

"Ah," Michael replied. "About ninety percent of the Jewish people in Lithuania were believed to have been murdered in the Holocaust. Those murdered souls would have left art, money, gold, jewelry behind for the Nazis to confiscate."

Ninety percent seemed like an incredibly high number and so she asked, "Did that ninety percent mean nine people died or a far bigger number? Nine is, nine too many, but it also represents the potential size of seized assets."

"It was perhaps 190,000 of 200,000 Jewish Lithuanians at the time on perhaps a total population of a little more than two million people," Michael said reading from a website on his computer.

"Wow, that's a horrible number, and it puts this part of Europe into perspective. I have to think there was a fair amount of loot from those murdered people," Jill replied, trying to imagine how horrible a time that was in the early 1940s. Then her logical mind took over, and she thought about the number of people it took to kill nearly 200,000 in three years. All she could do was shudder at the atrocity of it all. She wondered how they found enough men to kill their fellow citizens, but then she could think of wars over the centuries that had been equally brutal.

She tuned back into the conversation as Michael said, "And these pictures are from Latvia."

Jill returned her focus to Nick's emails. She'd read all that was available and while some of the English translations were awkward, she'd found nothing more than poor grammar catching her attention. How else could she look at the emails? How about the mention of Lithuania, Latvia, Poland, or a city therein? Another search turned up no mention of a Country or City. Her eyes went through the emails a third time, and she focused on the word "tallinn". She assumed it was a miss spelling the first few times, but when she re-read the sentence, it appeared to be a place. Was it a city, a park, a restaurant? A Google search led to a town in Estonia.

"Have you guys come across any pictures from Estonia?"

"Not, yet as we're still in Latvia," Nicole replied. "Why?"

"There's mention of a city named Tallinn in Nick's email and I looked up the word, and it's a city in Estonia."

Michael smiled at her, "Yes, I've been there. It's one of the oldest cities in Europe, and there are many art galleries there."

Jill wondered if she'd ever learn enough about the world at large, but then after a quick search, she found that her home State Of California had forty times the population of Estonia and ten times the square feet of Estonia. Since she hadn't visited Estonia she hadn't had the chance to learn its geography or cities. When she'd been in school, Estonia was a part of Russia adding to her memory banks of certain parts of the world. Oh well, back to the problem at hand - what did Tallinn have to do with this case if anything? And how about the mention of Scotland? If she were to have any impact on finding this treasure, it needed to be in Scotland, and more precisely near Edinburgh.

"Was Nazi gold rumored to be in any of the countries we've just spoken about?" Jill asked the two art experts.

"No, but these former Soviet States were controlled by the Nazis, so it's reasonable that they might contain Nazi stolen artifacts," Michael replied. "Conversely, all of the biggest art finds have been in Germany. So it's not clear that Hitler had the time or resources to move loot some twelve hundred kilometers northeast, but anything is possible."

Jill looked at the time and realized she'd been researching

Nick's communications for several hours. It was time to stretch and get a walk in before returning to her laptop.

She stood up and did a few stretches and said, "I've been sitting too long. I'm going to find lunch somewhere in Edinburgh and stretch my legs with a walk."

Nicole and Michael were deep into identifying pictures and briefly looked up and nodded.

Jill took her laptop upstairs and locked it and Nick's phone in her room safe. She then grabbed her purse, jacket, and sunglasses as it appeared to be sunny outside.

CHAPTER 28

ill walked about three blocks before she began looking for a place to have lunch. The first block seemed promising then the next two, not so much. She seemed to be in an older area with more houses than businesses and small alleys separating apartment blocks with few people out and about. They were probably all at work. She could see down the road another two blocks the beginning of a restaurant row, so she stayed on course as the exercise felt great. Looking in the distance, she could see the words pub and café, and she was sure one of them would have a menu item that appealed to her. She looked down each alley as she passed, and found children playing in one on bicycles with mothers nearby keeping them safe. Another alley was empty except for a parked scooter; she was crossing the third alley when she sensed someone behind her seconds before she felt her body jolt from a Taser gun. She tried to call out for help, but she couldn't coordinate her vocal cords to let out a scream.

The muscle shaking continued as she descended to the ground and then she lost track of time and place for a few moments while her body contended with muscle contractions.

As she became more aware of her surroundings, she looked around and found herself seated on the floor of what appeared to be a building under renovation. Where was she? She couldn't remember seeing a building like this before. Where was Nathan? Was she in Northern California, her home?

And then as if she put readers on to be able to see text, her vision and brain focused, and she had a clear picture.

She'd come into contact with a Taser of some sort, and it hadn't been enough to kill her, so whoever had done it hadn't wanted her dead. Nathan wasn't around to help as he was up north in Scotland visiting a distillery today. She felt for her purse which contained her cell phone but didn't sense it on her shoulder or at her side. Then she took another look around the room and spotted a man in his mid to late forties, dark hair with some grey, he had a round face and receding hairline and was holding a Taser in his hand.

"Voglio sapere che cosa sai di Nicholas," the man said.

Jill was trying to understand what language she was hearing - Spanish? Italian? Latin?, but who spoke Latin? She did hear the word Nicholas, so she assumed he was asking her a question about Nick.

"I don't understand you," Jill said. Then she added, "No hablo español Je ne parle pas français. " Those three sentences were the extent of her ability to tell the man she could not understand him.

He fired another sentence at her, and she just tried to look confused which wasn't much of an act on her part.

Since they were at a stalemate, she thought she'd see if she could walk out the door of this building, and so stood up, taking a moment for the dizziness to go away. When she headed for the door, he stood up, got in front of her and held up the Taser. Okay, Jill thought, he's not going to kill me, but he's not going to let me leave. They seemed to be at a stalemate as they hadn't found a common language.

He threw another sentence at her and again she didn't understand and repeated in English, "I don't understand what you said. I don't speak your language."

Again she made as if to leave and he gestured with the stun gun that it was a bad idea. She knew that such guns had ranges of up to twenty feet, so no matter how fast she ran, the room was too small for her to escape a stream of electricity.

She looked around again for her purse, and saw it near his feet, and so she said aloud, "Hey Siri, how do say in Italian I don't understand?"

Jill paused, and then Siri said, "I don't understand what you said."

Jill tried again, "How do you say in the Italian language I don't understand?"

Siri replied with, "Here take a look."

That wasn't going to do her a lick of good. The man had the look of a Spaniard or an Italian, but the only word she could think of was hello and thanks, so she tried them. "Ciao, grazie."

The man looked confused then understood what Jill was trying to do. So he said, "Si, Italian."

Okay, Jill thought at least she knew what language he was speaking, but she'd just used all of her capacity to speak in Italian. She tried, "Parle Anglais."

He nodded his understanding but was at a loss as to how to bridge their gap. Jill pointed to her purse and said "iPhone" and "telephono." She was beginning to feel like an idiot with her fake French or Italian and of course, that was better than feeling scared that this man was going to hurt her. Next, she would raise the volume of her voice in hopes that she would be understood.

He seemed to understand what she planned to do with her phone so they could understand each other. Jill noticed he had an old-fashioned flip phone on his belt, so they would need to use her phone's translate function. Her captor was wisely suspicious that she would just use the phone to call for help. Fortunately, despite the age of his phone, he didn't seem entirely clueless. He pulled her phone out of her purse, opened the Google app for translation. Unbeknownst to Jill, he had watched his brothers in Operation Gladio use it to speak with each other. He'd never needed it as everyone that ordered his plumbing services spoke Italian on Sardinia.

Soon they were communicating.

"What's your name?" Jill asked.

"That's not important. Tell me about Nicholas."

Jill thought "'tell you what about Nicholas?'

So she wrote back on the translation screen, "His favorite color was blue."

The man flashed angry eyes at her, and she shrugged, and then wrote on the screen, "What specifically do you want to know about Nick?"

His eyes cooled down a bit, and he replied, "Has Nicholas told you about the treasure?"

Jill was surprised by the question as that was precisely what she'd been searching for with Nicole and Michael, but she answered with the truth, "No he never mentioned a treasure or that he was even searching for something."

The man paused for a minute, apparently thinking, but Jill noticed his thumb was still on the stun gun switch, so she waited in silence.

"What did you tell the police about Nick and Girard? I saw you meeting with them."

This translation software was a pain for a more extended explanation such as what she now needed to provide.

"The police in Cardiff contacted us as Nick was meeting us there. There was a message on his phone about it. I'm a forensic pathologist, an expert in autopsies, so they invited me to participate in the examination of Nick's remains."

The man seemed to be processing that piece of information, and it was clear it wasn't the answer he expected. He thought for a while longer then typed in his next question.

"How did you meet Nicholas?"

"My friends and I were on vacation in Amsterdam, staying at a hotel he managed the security for and we were having problems with a few people following us. He interceded, and a friendship was born. We manage to meet once or twice a year."

Again it appeared her answer wasn't what the man expected. Jill weighed bringing up Operation Gladio, but decided she didn't know enough about the man's reaction to launch that bomb at him yet.

"Why did you ask me about a treasure? Did Nick mention he was searching for a treasure or your friend Girard, was he working with you to find a treasure? What kind of treasure – money, jewels, art?"

These long messages were boring to write; she wondered when he would let her go.

He ignored her questions and asked, "How long was Nick going to be staying with you?"

"About three or four days." Jill wondered what that had to do with anything. There was another silence as the man thought through her responses, so Jill wrote one more message on the phone.

"Can I leave now and go back to my hotel?"

There was another round of silence. This guy seemed like a slow thinker, or maybe he hadn't thought much beyond her kidnapping.

CHAPTER 29

Giovanni stared at the woman trying to decide what his next steps were. He'd planned to head home to Sardinia that evening. He was due at work tomorrow, but should he risk his job and see if this woman could tell him something about the treasure? Perhaps he would tell her of the other words that Girard mentioned before he died.

He'd made no progress in uncovering the alleged treasure that Girard spoke of, and unless he came up with some new information, there would be no reason to return to the United Kingdom or even hope for the reactivation of Operation Gladio. He felt weighted down by what he'd done less than an hour ago and with the weight of his next decision. Giovanni had never hurt another human being, and today he'd fired an electrical charge at a woman. How low could he go? He'd never been a leader before; he had always taken instructions from someone else and now he was frozen on what to do next.

After more thought, he decided to try the other words that he remembered from Girard and see if the woman could connect the dots for him.

"Do any of these words mean anything to you? Camp, quarry or quail, northern Europe or the UK?"

Jill sighed as she watched him type. He was typing more than a 'yes' or 'no'. She was convinced that he'd been about to let her go and then he began with typing a message that was clearly longer.

She looked at the words and tried to think back to her conversations with Nick. She couldn't remember Nick saying those words.

With the shake of her head and the word, 'no' typed on her phone screen, Giovanni felt like he'd hit the end of this road. He hung his head down depressed that he couldn't go any farther with the clues from Girard and Nick.

He was still holding Jill's phone, so he typed, "You can go now," as he pointed to the exit and reached out to hand her phone to her.

Jill accepted her phone back and saw his message with relief and debated asking the man to talk with Nicole and Michael. Perhaps one of them spoke Italian and could have a more thorough conversation with him. She could hear Nathan's voice in her head saying, 'Idiot get out of there and call the police,' but she couldn't do it. Okay maybe he wouldn't call her an idiot to her face, but that would definitely be his thinking. Yeah, the man had hurt her with the stun gun, her muscles had been in pain, but he'd made sure she didn't get hurt on her descent to the ground. She decided they might get farther with the treasure hunt if she included him in the conversation.

After hesitating another moment, she wrote a lengthy message about Nicole and Michael and suggested he might want to talk with them. She added that the treasure they were seeking would likely be returned to the families it had been stolen from and not to Giovanni personally.

He read her message and weighed his options. He'd decided to give up on the treasure, what would it hurt to talk to these people before he left for home? He sighed acknowledging his life inside

Operation Gladio was over. He looked over at Jill and nodded his agreement.

They walked out of the building and back to the hotel bar where Michael and Nicole were working. The two looked up at her and then their eyes widened in surprise at the new arrival she had in tow behind her.

"Do either of you speak Italian?"

Michael nodded, "I'm not as fluent in it as in other languages, but does he need directions? I can handle that, but I don't know much about where things are located in Edinburgh."

Jill smiled at Michael's misperception of the situation. She replied, "He's not looking for directions, rather he knows a little bit about the treasure that Nick might have located."

"Mein Gott," Michael said. Jill guessed that was a German exclamation for surprise.

Michael switched to Italian, introducing himself and Nicole. The three of them appeared deep in conversation with Michael vacillating between German for Nicole and Italian for Giovanni. Jill was disappointed that they hadn't asked where or how she'd met Giovanni, instead they'd immediately rushed into getting information. Jill just shrugged and decided she was in the mood for food and alcohol after her heart-pounding excitement of the past hour and left the bar for the second time for a meal.

After an uneventful lunch during which she relaxed and examined her actions that morning. She decided that a preponderance of people would deeply question her lack of desire to report a man who stun gunned her, to Scottish authorities. In fact, she hoped that her abductor would be gone by the time Nathan returned later that afternoon as she guessed that a meeting between the two of them would not go well. She'd head back to the hotel bar and see if Nicole and Michael had finished with the man from Italy.

CHAPTER 30

Jill got her wish as the bar contained only Nicole and Michael upon her return.

"Hey guys, did the man provide you with any useful information?" Jill asked.

"He really just confirmed the direction that we were taking was correct. We are following a trail as you know from Lithuania, north," Michael said. "I asked him more questions about his word 'treasure', but he didn't have a clue as to gold, jewels, art, or something else. He's left for the overnight train back to Sardinia. He refused to give us his name or contact information."

After a pause, Nicole asked, "Where did you meet him?"

Jill knew they would eventually ask that question and so she'd formulated an answer while at lunch.

"As I was looking for a place to dine, I made eye contact with him on the sidewalk and recognized him as the guy that had been at Edinburgh Castle, when the other guy tried to shove me over the castle wall," Jill said thinking back to those scary moments. "Were you in the vicinity when that occurred?"

"No, it took us a few days to find you in Edinburgh, and it was really dumb luck that had us crossing paths. You say that someone tried to push you over the castle wall? How terrifying! No wonder you were so suspicious of Michael and I. What happened?"

Jill explained what had happened at the castle and added, "I spoke with this man through translation software on my phone, so I didn't get the full story, but I had a feeling he was an acquaintance rather than a friend as he didn't seem particularly heartbroken over his death."

"I asked how he knew Nick, and he said that they belonged to a men's club, but that was all he would say. I wonder if they belonged to this Operation Gladio, you've mentioned?"

"Perhaps so. Given the guy's secrecy. Why else would he refuse to give us his name and contact information? So are you any farther along on guessing what the treasure is and where it might be?"

"We're farther ahead in that we have had confirmed for us that there was some kind of treasure that Nick was investigating and that we're looking in the right region."

"But having a region to look for treasure is like looking for a needle in a haystack as we Americans like to say. Besides he mentioned two regions to me - northern Europe and Northern U.K."

The two Germans looked at her, puzzled over her phrase. She started to explain when the picture became clear to them.

"Yes, it's like looking for a needle in a haystack," Michael agreed with a small smile. "But we've been successful in finding those needles in the past."

"Before I left for lunch, I asked if you'd come across any pictures from Estonia and you said not yet. Have you found any since? Have you found any pictures of Scotland?"

"Yeah, we did for Estonia. There was a picture of the Klooga train station," replied Nicole with excitement in her voice.

"I'm not familiar with that city, but you seem excited by your find. What's special about Klooga?" Jill asked.

"From a historical point, it's the rail station to which many

Jews were transported before arriving at the concentration camp there and losing their lives," replied Nicole.

"Yes, but it's unlikely they arrived with their treasures. Weren't many Jews forcibly removed from their homes? Sometimes allowed to bring a small suitcase with them. Neither of those scenarios seems like they could produce much treasure for the Nazis in Estonia. Wouldn't the treasure need to be moved into the country by the Nazis hoping to hide stuff until they could come back for it after the war's end?" Jill asked thinking about the strategy of the Nazis.

"This is true," Nicole said quietly, "but it's all we have at the moment."

"Perhaps there is no treasure despite what Nick seemed to have thought."

"If you believe that, you should leave us Nick's phone," Michael suggested.

"I'll definitely do that after his funeral next month, but for now, I'll hold on to the phone."

Jill was expecting a message from Nathan and so glanced down at her phone to see if it was from him. Instead, she was surprised by the message.

CHAPTER 31

*I*t was from Jo.

"You know me - I can never sleep on a plane and since it had Wi-Fi, I decided that I would look into your German mystery, rather than ruining my vacation glow by reading work emails, LOL."

Hallelujah, thought Jill. Jo had provided so many break-throughs by evaluating the finances of suspects. Admittedly she was curious about how good Jo would be in finding historical financial records, but she'd pulled off miracles in the past.

'The accounting records of the Nazis are immense and chaotic. I started with an overview of where the Nazis financed their war and what the rest of the world did after the war was over. Did you know there are fifteen million pages in our National Archives alone in addition to what the rest of the world has? No way am I wading through that pile of paper! So here's a summary; at one time the Germans had $580 million of gold that they used to finance the war. By the way, that's $5.6 billion in today's money. Germany bought raw materials from many countries like Turkey and Argentina to make stuff used in war. They also needed to pay for and care for their troops. The Nazis stole the money from countries that they took over as well as from victims of the

Holocaust. So now you know where the money came from and what it was used for. Switzerland was the banker for the Nazis - they stored the gold and dispersed monies for war purchases.'

Jill appreciated Jo's synopsis of the situation as she hadn't learned those details.

'I looked at many different documents including ledger books and other materials from the archives of history. Thankfully they put all of that stuff on the internet! Here's my conclusion from an accounting perspective - there is no pile of hidden gold from the Nazis anywhere but in a few small accounts in Swiss banks.

Yes, I'm betting my CPA accreditation on my conclusion. There still may be a treasure that Nick was looking for, but it won't be a large cache of gold. There are still missing works of art, but my advice is not to waste any time looking for a mythical gold train.'

Jo added a few more comments and ended the email. Jill leaned back and thought, 'now what?'

She looked up to find her German associates staring at her, and she blurted out, "Jo, my accounting friend, did an analysis of the income and expenses of the Nazis and believes there is no gold train, no missing and large stockpile of cash. And I believe her analysis, mostly because she's never been wrong."

Michael and Nicole looked at each other and then she replied, "Your friend is probably right. Given that the world has not discovered the legendary train despite the advanced technology at our disposal in over sixty years since it was rumored stolen. However, we have a sacred duty to discover and return all possessions looted by the Nazis, and we've traveled down many a dead end in our lives."

After a pause, Jill asked, "Or... might we be looking for a different treasure?"

"It's possible. Every time there's war in a region, treasures disappear, and Europe has seen many wars dating back thousands of years," Michael replied.

"Have you ever chased one of these other treasures?" Jill asked curious about their jobs.

"Mostly we've investigated and located paintings. We've handled a few sculptures and coins, also. We've never found gold bars as they are too easy to melt down and sell, rather than be returned to the rightful owners. I think in the decade or so that I've searched, I've come across at most two or three works of art that aren't paintings from the plunderers of war," Michael replied.

"Thinking back to our conversation with Nick, I don't believe he mentioned the Nazi gold. In fact, I can't remember his exact words as to the type of treasure he was curious about," Nicole mused looking at Michael for clarity.

Pausing a moment to think back, he slowly spoke, "Nick mentioned World War II not specifically gold. Our mysterious friend said a treasure in a quarry in northern Europe near concentration camps. There are items missing from the war still today that the average person would call a treasure."

"Don't forget he said it might also be camps, as in the outdoors, quail in addition to quarry, and northern UK in addition to Europe," Jill said.

"The Nazis hated the Impressionists, and so Monet and his brethren's paintings were banned from Germany and any one of those today would fetch tens of millions of dollars. There were other things as well," said Nicole. "The problem is that some things disappeared due to the bombing in an area and you never know if something is hidden by a collector, stored in a tunnel, in a museum's back dusty storage room, or destroyed by a bomb."

"Yeah, there's the Amber Room from Russia. A few of the original stones have been found, but not the entire room which the Germans were known to have boxed up for transport back to Germany."

Jill paused a moment to look up the Amber Room and thought, 'wow how do you pack up a room like that without damaging it?' And then said to the two art experts, "So it was located in Saint

Petersburg, which isn't that far from Northern Europe? That seems probable location-wise."

"Yes, but it was also rumored to have been destroyed by the Royal Air Force and the Russians when they blew up Konigsberg Castle. Another rumor was that it was shipped to Poland only to be torpedoed in the Baltic Sea," noted Michael.

"Any other treasures that you can think of? Perhaps something from World War I or the Russian Revolution?" Jill asked. "Have you finished cataloging Nick's pictures? Is there anything new from Estonia or Scotland? Is there anything in those pictures that would make you think they were taken for a purpose other than a vacation picture?"

There was silence while they thought about the pictures. Michael pulled up a picture and a discussion ensued with Nicole. The two of them did this for a few minutes, and Jill decided to leave them to their own conversation and pulled up her email. There was a note from Nathan that he would be back at the hotel in an hour and he had some exciting news. There was also a second email from Jo.

'Thinking back on our two-plus years with Nick, he was full of gallantry and so I could see a stay-behind army appealing to that gallant side of his personality. I could also see him searching for treasure confiscated by the Nazis, as again he would feel chivalrous in returning it to the rightful owners. I also don't see him wasting time by chasing ridiculous legends like the Nazi gold. I think he saw a painting somewhere and guessed it to be expensive...just my thoughts.'

Jill checked her watch and thought Jo would be in the air a while longer and thus have an internet connection. So she sent a reply with the words given them by the Italian man. She left out the full story as there was no sense in distracting Jo, but maybe she would make something of the word association. She'd give her ten to twenty minutes for a response. Meanwhile, she tuned back into Michael and Nicole's conversation.

"Anything?" she asked.

They looked up at her and shook their heads.

"Jo thinks Nick is the type to chase a noble objective like returning a treasure to the original owner. I sent her the words of our Italian guy to see if they mean anything to her."

Soon there was a response, from Jo,

The words don't bring anything of meaning to me, but I thought of something else. Do you think the Scottish police would let you see the cell phone of the man that tried to push you off the castle wall? Maybe there's a matching picture or something else to direct your search?'

Wow, that was a brilliant suggestion. Why hadn't she thought of it? She replied her thanks and searched her purse for the card of Detective Inspector Campbell and dialed his number. After a lengthy conversation, he agreed to allow Jill to view the phone. Glancing at her watch, she knew Nathan would arrive at any moment, and she needed to get there before the Detective Inspector left for the day.

It was about two miles away as the crow flies, but the castle stood between her hotel and the police station, so she'd grab a cab. Looking up at Michael and Nicole, she said, "I met Detective Inspector Campbell after the man tried to push me over the castle walls; he investigated the case. He's agreed to let me view the man's cell phone, and we have reason to believe that he knew of whatever treasure Nick was searching for. I'm going to try, and take a picture of everything I find on the phone and I'll share with you."

"Can we join you at the police station?" Nicole asked.

"No. The detective was very specific; he indicated that I should leave the other members of my team behind. My request was unusual, and I think if he has too much time to think about it, he'll change his mind and deny my viewing the phone."

"Will you at least take one of our phones and take pictures with it?" Michael asked.

"I'll take it, but if I'm pressed for time and it takes too long to snap pictures with two different cell phones, I'll rely strictly on my phone. Any last minute advice on what I should look for?"

Nicole and Michael both replied at the same time with the word, "Painting". Then Michael gave Nicole the go ahead and she added, "Sculpture, coins, jewelry."

CHAPTER 32

*J*ill nodded and left the bar heading to the hotel lobby to call a cab. She ran into Nathan just entering the lobby.

He walked over to her for a quick hug and kiss and said, "Hey babe, have I got stories to tell you."

Jill smiled and thought, wait till you hear my story about being kidnapped. Instead, she said, "I need to run over to the Police Scotland building. Detective Inspector Campbell has agreed to let me examine the cell phone from the guy that tried to push me over the castle wall. Can I catch up with you in an hour or two?"

"Why don't I come along," Nathan suggested, turning to head for the exit.

"When the detective agreed to let me examine the phone, he specifically said I could not bring anyone with me, and I want to hurry and get there before he has time to think and change his mind."

"What if the phone's locked?"

That question stopped Jill in her tracks.

"Then I guess I'm screwed as Henrik's niece has returned to Germany," Jill said as she leaned in to kiss Nathan goodbye before moving towards the exit. She waved at him and added, "I should be back in about two hours at the most," as she disappeared through the exit door.

'Oh well', thought Nathan. His new information about her case would have to wait until she returned. Maybe he'd stop in and see what Michael and Nicole were up to while he waited for Jill's return.

Jill found a taxi outside and entered the vehicle saying "14 St. Leonard's Street."

After a short ride, she arrived at police headquarters. A man at the entry desk directed her to the second floor unit of the Specialist Crime Division as the location for DI Campbell.

Clearly, DI Campbell had been notified of her arrival, as he was waiting for her when the elevator door opened.

"Dr. Quint, I didn't think I would see you again as the murder of your friend was solved."

"Well, yes, we know who murdered Nick and who tried to kill me, but we don't know the motive and that's been bothering me," Jill said thinking she would lose her stellar reputation as a forensic pathologist if he found out she was looking for some treasure legend.

He stared at her as if trying to decipher what she was thinking, so she asked, "Do you know the motive for my friend's murder?"

"No, and it's not in my jurisdiction. The attempted murder of you is related to your relationship with the murder victim in Cardiff, but what exactly in that relationship made you a target, I'll never know without interviewing our dead suspect which I can't do. There was nothing in his possession that clued us into his thinking. Does it bother you not knowing his motive?"

"No," Jill replied. She added, "It doesn't change the fact that the suspect is dead and I have no further worries."

"Then why are you here? Why are wanting to see his phone? I am a detective you know, and your explanation seems weak. I know I wouldn't waste my time on a vacation in California trying to figure out a suspect's motive, so there must be more to the story, than you're telling me."

"You're an excellent detective, and I'm not willing to share my reasons with you because it has zero relation to Scotland and I don't want my reputation as a knowledgeable private investigator to be tarnished by my answer. Let me say, I'm on as we say in the States, 'a wild goose chase' that I'm too embarrassed to share with a formidable Detective Inspector such as yourself," Jill said holding out air quote marks with her hands.

"You Yanks are really full of bull aren't you?" he replied. "I have a full caseload, so I'll let it go, but don't hesitate to call if you need help." Then pulling a cellphone out of his pocket, he directed her towards a small room and handed her the phone once she was inside.

"You've got one hour, and that's it," Campbell said and turned to leave.

"Did the man have a family? I'm wondering why you still have the cell phone?" Jill asked just thinking of the question.

"Like your friend, he seems to have no family, or at least not one that we've located so far."

"Hmmm, that's unusual. What are the odds of two men having no family? In the case of our friend we simply were missing his full name, although once we had that, he still had no family. How odd!"

"Yes, well I'll leave you to the phone," DI Campbell said as he closed the door to the room that he'd shown Jill to.

'Okay, here comes the moment of truth,' thought Jill. Was the phone locked? The man worked for a secret organization, but then she thought he was rather stupid for trying to push her off the castle wall not seeing his own peril flying at him. She'd bet that the phone was unlocked.

She pressed the on button, but nothing happened. Great the battery was dead. She looked into the package that DI Campbell had handed her, but there was nothing more inside. She got up to exit the room only to find she was locked in. Okay, this must be an interrogation room used for suspects. She knocked on the door but no one came. So she went back to her purse and pulled out her cell phone and called the DI. Explaining her two problems he apologized for forgetting the door was locked and promised to round up the chargers from his fellow DIs and bring them to her. She was hoping that Scotland as a part of the European Union would have similar technology for charging cell phones. A few minutes later he appeared with several chargers and a spare key so she wouldn't find herself locked in again.

Fortunately, one of the chargers fit, and he left to return the others to his co-workers. Again, the anticipation ramped up inside her as she hit the power button after plugging in the phone. The phone went through its start-up machinations and then came alive to Jill's huge grin.

The phone was unlocked.

She looked at the emails first, and like Nick's phone, they were in at least two languages. After a quick test, she could find no easy way to forward all of the emails, so she left them and moved on to the texts and what she saw there excited her.

There was a string of texts involving a photo, but it was no ordinary photo. It was a photo of a painting of a public square, probably in Venice, and from Jill's uneducated eye, perhaps seventeenth or eighteen century. Yes, this might be the treasure.

She couldn't figure out how to forward the series of texts to herself, in part because the options on the phone were in Italian she guessed. So she took a photo of the texts related to the painting. From there she used Google to translate the word 'photo' into Italian and soon found herself scrolling through the phone for the word 'fotografie'. Landing on the photo section of Girard's phone, she began taking photos with her cellphone of his photos from about twenty photos before the Venetian painting to about twenty photos after. No sooner had she finished, then the door opened, and DI Campbell entered to say he was being called out on a case and he needed to return the phone to the evidence room.

Jill stood up handing him the phone, "Thank you for letting me view Mr. LeRoux's phone."

Clearly, the DI was in a hurry to get to his crime scene as he said, "I need to return this phone, can you find your way out of the building?"

"Yes."

They parted ways, and Jill approached the elevator she'd arrived on when the DI called out from the other end of the corridor, "Oh and Dr. Quint, I hope you'll brief me sometime soon over what you're looking for," and then he disappeared through a doorway.

Jill mumbled, "Not unless I need to as my reputation would suffer if there wasn't really a treasure here."

Twenty minutes later she was back in the hotel. She briefly glanced in the bar but didn't see Nathan there, so she took the stairway to their room and after unlocking the door found the room empty. She pulled out her phone to text him as perhaps he went to another place with Nicole and Michael as they hadn't been in the bar either. They would have a lot in common she thought with the art world.

He replied that he was indeed with the two Germans, two blocks away in an Irish pub. Address in hand, she headed out the door to meet them.

CHAPTER 33

She found them with beers, enjoying watching a musical group set-up for that evening's performance. The pub was loud and with music later, there would be no chance for conversation.

After exchanging pleasantries, Nicole asked, "Did you find something?"

"The Mother Lode, I think, as they say in the United States."

The two Germans looked at her in puzzlement and then thinking through her words Michael smiled and said, "Oh, you mean you found a gold mine."

"Yes," Jill replied. "Take a look at this," she said holding out a photo on her phone of the painting on Girard's phone.

Michael muttered something in German and then added, "Yes indeed the Mother Lode. That's Canaletto's Piazza San Margherita, missing since 1940 when the painting's owner fled Amsterdam. It's one of the most famous paintings still missing. On today's art auction market, it probably has a value of about nine million euros, which is about ten million I believe in United States dollars. In the nearly eighty years since WWII, there have been rumors of the painting's sightings, but all leads in the past have led nowhere."

"Would Nick or Girard have been able to sell the painting?" Nathan asked.

"No, it's registered with a site that tracks stolen Nazi artifacts," Nicole said. "Of course they could likely find an off-office market site and sell them for perhaps eighty percent of the painting's value to a private collector."

"So where is this painting?" Nathan asked.

"I don't know," Jill replied, "But I took a picture of the text message that includes the picture. The message is in the Guernésiais language, and I didn't want to take the time to translate it. I also took photos of the before and after photographs to see if we could identify the location."

Michael rubbed his palms together and said, "Finally, a solid clue. This picture is exciting!"

"Why? We don't know where in the world this painting is located," Nathan said.

"We know the painting exists and that fact by itself is important," Nicole replied. "Just having a recent photograph of the painting is proof that it exists; the mobile phone containing that photo was likely manufactured in the last five years or so. Would you agree with that?"

Both Jill and Nathan nodded.

"So now we move into finding where this painting is located," Michael suggested. "That is if you're interested in the search Dr. Quint? We would love to have you join as you have skills and technology we don't."

"We're due to fly home in about thirty-six hours, and we both have commitments at home. I'll join you in the search up until I'm scheduled to leave Scotland. Nathan, you have appointments tomorrow, and rather than joining you in the distillery tours and viewing more of this lovely country, I'll stay here and work with Nicole and Michael."

Nathan looked mostly resigned at her response. She was a bloodhound when sniffing a mystery. Besides she'd hit her limit in whiskey tasting. He had two appointments tomorrow that he didn't want to miss – he was meeting with the artist that designed the labels for the most prominent distillery in Scotland in the morning. It was Shangri-La for him, basically meeting a contemporary in a similar field. In the afternoon, he was meeting with another distillery that was considering hiring him to design their labels. It would be another venture into spirits label design, and he had a feeling that the morning meeting would give him a better appreciation for the afternoon meeting. He would have liked to have Jill along with him for the company, but he admitted she would have had significant time to kill during his two meetings.

He nodded his agreement, "Yes that will work." Jill's beer arrived, and they settled into a conversation about the painting. Michael and Nicole took turns giving details about the painting, the artist, and the gallery owner that fled Amsterdam. The owner had died a decade ago, but there were still heirs that had rightful ownership of the painting. Jill had seen a Canaletto painting in the Getty Museum when she lived in Los Angeles, and she really liked the artist for his realistic portrayals of Saint Mark's Square in Venice. The art historians educated her in that period of art, and she felt like she had a private docent tour of the artwork of the Venetian paintings.

After finishing dinner, they walked back to the hotel. Nathan settled an arm around Jill's neck, and she winced hoping that he didn't notice her discomfort. It seemed that the area between her neck and shoulder was sore from where the Italian man had shocked her that afternoon. She'd have to look in the mirror to see if there was a mark. She knew she might have a burn where the electrical charge touched her skin. They got back to their hotel room, and Jill made use of the bathroom before heading down to the hotel pub to work with her German colleagues. She glanced in the mirror and was not surprised to see a burn mark.

She supposed she owed Nathan an explanation before he discovered the mark on his own.

She exited the bathroom and walked over to the sofa where Nathan was sketching a label. Sometimes he was working on a project for a client and other times he was just doodling. She sat down next to him and he looked up surprised. He'd thought she'd rush down to the pub to search for the painting.

"I haven't taken the opportunity to tell you about something that happened during my lunch break," Jill said tentatively.

There must have been something in her voice as he looked at her suspiciously.

She decided to tell the whole story in a rush and then wait for him to ask questions or criticize her actions.

"I was tasered by an Italian guy that was a friend of Girard LeRoux and likely Nick. The Germans spoke with him, and he offered some clues as he knew both Nick and Girard were hunting for a treasure, but he didn't know what kind of treasure. He's left and gone back to Italy."

Nathan stood there mute from all the emotions roiling through him. He tried to focus on the most important question which was, "Were you injured?"

"Not really. He made sure I didn't injure myself when I crumbled to the ground. I think I might have a small burn from the electrical charge, but it's fine."

"So why don't the police have him in custody?"

"Because I didn't call them and report the incident."

"Why?" Nathan asked though he wanted to ask other questions.

"In part because I wanted Michael or Nicole to interview him about Nick and Girard. You know I don't speak Italian, so I had to use my phone to translate; thus we had a very rudimentary conversation. Michael speaks Italian and so spoke with him at length, then he left."

"Did you learn anything from him?"

"He had keywords that don't necessarily make sense-Northern Europe or UK, treasure, quarry or quail, and concentration camp or just camp. I'm not sure where the words came from perhaps Michael knows."

"Why didn't you call the police while he was speaking to Michael? You had the perfect opportunity."

"It seemed a complication that would interfere with our vacation. He did his best to make sure I wasn't hurt, he mostly seemed sad that I didn't have secret information from Nick for a treasure of some sort. I guess they weren't very good at sharing the secret between this man, Girard and Nick."

"How did you explain your meeting him to Michael and Nicole?"

Jill thought that this was going better than hoped. She'd expected Nathan to be angry that she hadn't immediately called for help, but he seemed to be handling her explanation well.

"I told them I recognized him from the castle and that we chatted but I was having a hard time communicating given the language barrier, so after I introduced them I left the hotel for lunch and a large glass of wine."

"Dr. Quint, you do some amazing things," he said leaning over to kiss her.

She returned the kiss grateful that he wasn't angry with her decision making. It's what made her love him; he took the time to reason through decisions rarely letting his emotions dictate his responses.

She thought it was best to move on and so said, "Thanks. I'm going to drop off my stuff and head back to the pub downstairs to see if we can figure out where this priceless painting is."

He watched her leave the room, worried about her safety, yet in the time he'd known her she dodged many a bullet so to speak. He was hurt when she first mentioned the incident; hurt that she hadn't told him earlier, but he supposed he was partially responsible for that as they hadn't had a moment alone until just now and he had to agree with her reasoning for not contacting the police. It would add more complications and add nothing to their treasure search. Besides the guy, in the end, did little harm to Jill. He thought he'd look up taser gun side effects, but he was pretty sure, that Jill's only injury was the small skin burn.

CHAPTER 34

Jill entered the pub and joined Michael and Nicole who had been speaking in German huddled over Michael's computer.

"Did you guys locate the painting?"

Nicole shook her head 'no' and added, "We were speculating on where it might be, and we couldn't think of a location that it can't be. An art collector could have taken it anywhere in the world."

"Unless it was moved in say the last month, the painting needed to be in a location that both Nick and Girard visited."

"True," Michael said, "but how do we know where they've been?"

Jill thought for a while and said, "I have Nick's passport among his personal effects. Let me get it and check the countries he's visited recently."

"He won't have gotten a pass if he moved among the Schengen countries," Nicole said.

"What's a Schengen country?" Jill asked having never heard of the term.

"European Union countries," Nicole said.

"Oh, ok, you're right that he wouldn't have a passport stamp likely for much of his travels. Still, let me see what he has. It will at least document his travels in the UK, right?"

"Yeah," Michael said.

Jill left to gather Nick's passport and returned to the bar moments later while opening the passport to read the country stamps. It was five years old and she located the United States stamp from when he visited them in Colorado to help work on a case.

His recent activity included three trips to the UK, including twice entering Scotland at the Edinburgh Airport passport control. That was curious, Jill thought.

Looking at Michael and Nicole, she said, "It's rather odd that he's had three crossings into the UK over the last three months or so. Odd because I'm not aware of any business or family interests in Scotland. I'll check with someone in his company to see if they we're negotiating an account here in Scotland."

"Do you have the dates of the various pictures on Girard's phone? That will clue us in on their movements."

"Unfortunately, I don't remember if the dates were labeled. He had a different model of a phone than the one I use," Jill said thinking about getting another view of the phone. To help her make a decision on the next step, she asked Nicole, "Tell me about the legal process you go through from discovering a stolen Nazi artifact? How do you actually identify and acquire it."

For the next ten minutes, Jill listened to the two art experts describe a process that varied from case to case, but she heard a constant in it that she wanted to use now for this case.

"I think I should contact DI Campbell of Police Scotland for his help. I think we could get some information on Nick's movements here."

She heard her phone beep and noted the response from one of Nick's employees. She was unaware of any negotiations anywhere in the UK.

"Usually we bring the police in after we've located the artwork, but this is a different case, so let's see if they have an interest to join our search when we don't know if the treasure is inside Scotland," Michael said.

Jill looked at the time and found it to be approaching nine at night. Too late to call the detective on his personal cell phone with a non-emergency question, so she chose his office phone and left a message.

"I'll see if he calls me back in the morning," Jill said. Tomorrow was her last full day in Scotland, so it was now or never for DI Campbell to render assistance if he was interested.

Michael and Nicole just shrugged and said, "You're the expert about the police. Personally, I've never dealt with Police Scotland, so I appreciate your knowledge and connection. So should we just hang out here in the bar in the morning and wait to hear from you?"

Jill thought a few moments and shook her head, "Do whatever you want in the city. If the Detective Inspector wants to assist, we'll go to him, and his building is about twenty minutes from here so just stay in a thirty-minute radius of 14 St. Leonard's Street and I'll keep you posted."

They shortly said their 'goodnights' and departed from the bar.

Nathan looked up in surprise when she entered the room. She was back at least an hour earlier than he expected.

"You're back early. Did you find the location of the painting and call it a night?"

"Yeah, right. It was that easy," Jill said with a mocking grin. "No, I contacted DI Campbell for his help, so we'll see where that goes in the morning."

"So you're not going to the distilleries with me?"

"I don't know; it'll depend on the DI's response. Would you be terribly disappointed?"

"Yes and no. It's a beautiful country, and we might have found the Loch Ness Monster while we traveled north to one of the distilleries. I'd also be pretty proud of you if you locate a ten million dollar painting stolen from a family by the Nazis. That would be special for the family, and the publicity wouldn't hurt your reputation as a private detective."

"I don't do these jobs to bolster my reputation, but you're right it will be a positive mark on my resume. We'll have the motive for Nick's murder and that's important too.

"If you get involved in the case, I could cancel my appointments and stick around Edinburgh and explore whiskey and beer since I'm always looking for new ideas. I can always come back and meet them later."

Jill sat next to him on the sofa and leaned in to kiss him, "You're such a sweetheart to tolerate my vacation disruptions with such good cheer. Guess that's part of why I love you; you let me be me."

"Actually, it works both ways. I have an endless capacity to explore wineries, breweries, and distilleries, so as long as you abandon me near one of them, it's almost as enjoyable as being in your company."

"Almost?"

"I can't hug, kiss, or neck with a wine barrel or whiskey keg."

Jill poked him in the ribs for his verbal jab and they proceeded to wrap up their nightly rituals, and fall into bed for bedtime play.

CHAPTER 35

Jill had awoken at her usual early hour, showered and dressed, and took her laptop to the hotel bar. She hadn't come up with any brilliant ideas overnight on how to find the painting's location. So instead she caught up on news and information from the California Winegrowers Association. It refreshed her brain to read about grape varietal production and new techniques for organic pest control, a particular passion of hers. She was so deeply immersed in an article on nitrogen production by crops pollinated by bees, that she likely missed the first vibrations from her cell phone. She'd been thinking instead of how to plant the perfect vegetable garden to create the nitrogen for her grape vines.

She picked up her phone looking at the area code and thought it might be DI Campbell returning her call.

"Hello."

"Dr. Quint, this DI Campbell returning your call. You say you have a question about a lost artwork. Can you explain?"

"Are you in your office? I'd rather meet you in person."

She heard a sigh at the other end as he said, "I am at the moment, but I might not be in an hour. So make it quick."

"I'll be there in less than twenty," Jill replied ending the call.

She texted Nathan to notify him of her departure as well as Nicole and Michael. It was still not quite eight, and so they were likely still in their rooms. She put her stuff in her bag and hefted it on her shoulder to walk outside and hail a cab, when at the door, Michael and Nicole appeared in a brisk walk, startled when they ran into her.

"This is good timing, we thought we were behind you," Nicole said, then added. "Good morning and what's the plan with the detective?"

Kudos to the Europeans for remembering their manners, Jill thought.

They found a cab outside, and the three filed into the rear with Jill giving the cabbie the address.

"Good morning to you as well. The detective returned my call, and I asked if I could see him in person regarding a stolen artwork. He said he might not be available in an hour, so we better make it quick. So I texted Nathan, then you two, gathered up my belongings and now you're caught up with my morning. My only strategy thus far was to have a face to face conversation to show him stuff."

Nicole looked encouragingly at Jill with a smile and said, "Yes, that's a good start."

"DI Campbell generously allowed my viewing of the cell phone yesterday. I say generously because he let me view it without my having provided a full explanation or justification first. So I think my plan is to perform introductions of you two first which helps legitimatize our search. Then I think I'll connect it to Nick and the gentleman yesterday, and end with showing him the picture to see if he's seen it. How's that sound?"

"He's our last angle to try. I mean you could publish a picture of the painting in the major Scottish newspapers and ask people if they saw the painting but sometimes that makes the owner hide their painting and sends you on the trail of false leads and I'm not aware of any other leads we haven't already pursued."

"Okay, then I'll keep my fingers crossed that this effort yields our painting. I'm flying home tomorrow, so it's today or you two will have to solve the case."

After arriving at the police station, they were shown into the same room that Jill had used the night before to view Girard LeRoux's cell phone. Jill performed introductions between the Germans and the DI which set his eyebrows upwards.

"Art recoverers, huh? Don't think I've run into that occupation before. How many pieces of art have you recovered?" DI Campbell asked suspiciously.

"We work for Brisdale's with our time split between researching the provenance of auction items and hunting for stolen artifacts of Nazi Germany. To answer your question we've returned four items to families primarily through our provenance work."

"So let me back up a moment and confirm that you would handle an artwork worth say ten million pounds?" Jill asked DI Campbell.

"Actually I was a part of the team that made the arrests for the theft of Leonardo Da Vinci's painting Madonna with the Yarnwinder worth four times the price of the estimated value of an artwork you mention in your voicemail. So yes, I'm your man for art theft. Now would you explain yourselves? I'm having trouble connecting the dots between two murders in Scotland and Wales, German art experts, and an American Physician."

"And Private Detective," Jill added. "I've got my license now."

The detective was not amused by Jill's last sentence. She shrugged and began the story for the detective.

"While the murderer of our friend was identified and accounted for, my friends and I wanted to understand the why of his murder. We owed that to him. After lots of research, we believe he and Girard LeRoux and an Italian man belonged to a stay-behind army from WWII."

"They're not old enough to have served and who's the Italian man?" Campbell interrupted. Intrigued with the start of the story, but only believing it because of the credibility of Jill Quint.

"I'll get to that. You can look in newspaper archives and find stories on stay-behind armies. It's not important to this art theft. We think that subsequent generations of stay-behind army members had little to do as there's little communism to prevent in the world. A side job of theirs may have been to recover stolen art. This is all speculation and what we've been able to put together talking to the Italian man and reading Nick's texts and emails. We think he and Girard might have discovered a painting located in Scotland that was registered on the list of stolen Nazi art. We think there was a disagreement as to what to do with the art that leads to Nick being pushed off Cardiff Castle."

"Who's the Italian guy?" asked Campbell again.

"Yesterday when I took a break from researching what the 'hidden treasure' might be and exited my hotel for lunch, once I traveled a few blocks, an Italian man came up behind me and hit me with a jolt of current from a taser gun."

"Did you report this to the police?"

"No," Jill said holding her hand up. "Other than the unpleasantness of the electrical jolt, he didn't hurt me. We had a discussion using my phone translator feature, and then I took him back to Nicole and Michael as Michael speaks Italian to see what his full story on the treasure might be."

Campbell was just looking at her with disgust said, "The very act of owning let alone hitting you with a stun gun is illegal in Scotland. Your Italian man should be in prison for the next five years in Scotland."

"Well it's too late, he left last night to return to Italy. I don't know his name or which city he is from, so let's move on."

"Were you burned by the electrodes?"

"A small burn on the back of my neck; look we're wasting time. I'm fine, the Italian man has left the United Kingdom, so let's worry about the art."

There was just silence as Jill was hit by waves of anger coming from DI Campbell. Then abruptly he exited the room. She looked at Michael and Nicole whose mouths had dropped open in astonishment and shrugged.

"You're a calm one!" Nicole exclaimed and after a pause added, "Should we leave?"

"Let's wait a bit and see what happens. Maybe he stepped out to cool his temper down. Besides, I think the door is locked."

After about five minutes Campbell returned with a woman.

"This is DI Murray, she worked on the last large art heist in Scotland," Campbell said as he made introductions. The detective was tall with thick gorgeous red hair pulled back in a ponytail. Freckles covered her face, and Jill bet she'd weakened many a criminal with her good guy persona.

"Do you have a picture of what you are searching for?" Murray asked.

Jill opened her laptop and brought up a picture of the Canaletto painting of San Margherita square in Venice.

"I've seen that picture somewhere, though not recently, maybe in my childhood," Murray said.

"Where did you see it?" all four people tried to ask the same question at the same time.

"Let me think," Murray said staring at the photo.

There was silence in the room while she stared at the computer screen with Campbell, while Jill, Michael, and Nicole stared at the detectives.

"I think I've seen it too. Where did you get this picture?" Campbell asked.

"From the cell phone of Girard LeRoux," Jill replied.

"Let me get the phone, and we'll look at what's on either side of the picture," Campbell said.

"I took pictures of that last night. I can show you on my laptop."

Campbell just stared at her and then muttered, "Ok then."

Jill showed the detectives pictures on either side of the painting. Then she set it on rotation so that the three images rotated every five seconds. Again the two detectives stared trying to remember where they had seen the painting.

DI Murray looked at DI Campbell and asked, "Could they be from summer camp as a wee child? Did we play on islands in the firth?"

"Maybe we went there for summer camp. My own wee ones went to soccer camp last summer. They don't seem to have the types of camps I went to as a wee one anymore. Now there has to be goals attached to the camp," Campbell replied.

"I remember visiting an island during one of my camps, and we scampered all over some rocks. One of my mates stumbled and left his skin behind on the island. Now you get sued for something like that as the parent removes their child from such a bad camp, but I just have fond memories."

"Maybe that's where we saw the painting as I have vague memories of an island visit."

"How about the islands you can see from Edinburgh castle? Might any of them contain a painting? Are any of them inhabited?" Jill asked.

"Not really," replied DI Murray. "How about Loch Lomond? It's a large lake that contains several islands, and I do remember one summer camp there."

"Maybe we should call our parents to see if they remember where they sent us to camp," Campbell proposed.

"Okay, I'll give mine a call."

The two detectives stepped out of the room to make calls to their respective parents. Knowing they would quickly get into a personal discussion, they wanted privacy.

Jill meanwhile was looking up Scottish islands as they spoke.

By the time the two detectives returned she lined up four islands in the firth and three in Loch Lomond. Could they visit seven islands in one day? Would the two detectives escort them? They might have bigger fish to fry in regards to crime. She decided to drop a text to Nathan that they might be making that trip to Loch Lomond after all.

CHAPTER 36

The two detectives returned to the room with a third person. Introduced as their superior, Detective Chief Superintendent Craig and quickly brought him up to date on the problem.

"Both Murray and I checked with our parents, but they don't remember where we went to camp."

"While you were out of the room, I think I might have narrowed our search down to seven islands," Jill said. "Perhaps we can discuss their merits."

Craig raised his eyebrows with a variety of emotions flaring behind his steel-rimmed glasses, but then he nodded and said, "Go ahead."

"Let's start with Loch Lomond. I'm sure you know much more about the lake then I do, so pardon me if any of this is repetitive. There is a building on each of the named islands that might contain a painting. By this I mean, they are not ruins which would ruin a painting. Also, the fact that Mr. LeRoux had a picture on his phone means there must be some way for the public to reach the island. "

"How did either man Mr. LeRoux or Mr. Brouwer know to visit the island?" Campbell asked. "It's not as if any of them are on anyone's bucket list."

Now Nicole spoke up for the first time, "When we met with Nick, he asked us many questions about stolen Nazi loot - where it was found, etc. Most art that has been already recovered came from Germany and Austria which are obvious locations. Presently, there is known stolen art in most of the major museums of the world and different plans are being worked out to return the pieces or their monetary value to the descendants of the original owners. At this point major works are hidden from the public view in private collections or in locations deserted shortly after World War II. Do any of the islands fit either description? Perhaps he had a lead to an island in Scotland and then spent a couple of trips searching those islands."

The screen had continued playing the before and after pictures to the painting, while they were in the room. Now Craig was clearly taken in by the photos knowing like the other two that he'd seen the location at some time.

"Ms. Quint, can you stop the loop of pictures? I want to study those pictures."

Jill did as he requested and they all watched him flip the pictures at his own speed.

"Sir, I think it has to be Loch Lomond or the Firth as Campbell and I have both seen the painting, and we both think it was in our childhoods. Those are the only two water locations I went to as a young child."

"Perhaps we can enlarge the wall behind the painting and tell if it is concrete or wood, that might narrow the choices," Campbell suggested.

What did you say the value of the painting was?" Craig asked.

"Perhaps nine to ten million Euros," Michael replied.

"Do you have any security camera footage of the roads to Loch

Lomond and the Firth to see if Mr. LeRoux or Nick is spotted on them?" Jill asked.

"We have about two hundred cameras stationed around Edinburgh, but as you can imagine that creates a lot of footage and therefore we only store for thirty-one days. Do you think they visited any of these islands in the last thirty-one days?"

Jill nodded, "The dates on Mr. LeRoux's camera are within those dates, and I can't imagine they would just sit on an expensive piece of art for months."

"Because the two men in question are deceased, we won't need a court order to look at the footage, but it could take us days to get back the results as we're looking at nearly one hundred-fifty thousand hours of footage," Craig warned.

Jill saw other holes in this approach such as Nick's or Girard's faces being clear to a CCTV camera. Indeed if they drove there in the dark, their faces wouldn't be visible.

"Perhaps my friend Nathan, Michael, Nicole, and I could just have Scotland's permission to visit all seven locations today. I return to the U.S. tomorrow and the search can continue without me beyond that."

"Just a minute," said DCS Craig as he indicated for Murray and Campbell to precede him from the room.

"We'll need to rent a boat in both locations; this Loch Lomond and the fifth," Michael suggested.

"It's Firth, not fifth though I admit that it's hard to hear sometimes with their accents," Jill said. "Let's see what they come back with. I have a feeling we're going to get some help. I just want to get a move on. I'm going to call Nathan and see if he wants to join us."

Jill reached Nathan and was pleased to hear he was about to take a cab to her location, ready to join the trip to some Scottish islands.

The door opened, and the DCS and one of his detectives returned.

"Campbell is making arrangements for a boat at Loch Lomond and Firth. You'll have a van and two of my detectives to find the painting today. If you don't find it, the case will likely be reassigned to our cold case division, and you are not to search for it on your own. If you do find it and it's on private property, then the detectives will confiscate it while we get a court order after one of your two art experts verifies it's the original stolen piece of art. Can you do that?"

"No," said Michael. "I can verify that it is the Canaletto that is on the missing art list. But I'll need to test the canvas' age, x-ray the picture, and do an analysis of the pigments to verify its authenticity."

"Well, maybe I'll contact the National Museum of Scotland to see if they can lend a hand. I'll worry about that if you find it," Craig said. "Good luck," he muttered then shook their hands and left the room.

"We're going to find it today," Nicole said. "I can just feel that we're on the verge of a big discovery."

"We'll see," Jill said. "I'm glad I have the right shoes on to clamber over islands today, and the weather report said it will remain dry today! It'll be a unique twist on tourism."

Michael and Nicole offered her a small smile as Nathan was shown into the room. Smart man that he was, he arrived carrying a heavier jacket for Jill. As being out in the open water was likely a colder climate then downtown Edinburgh.

Jill provided Nathan with an update on their island tour showing him and the two Germans, a general map of where they were going. From what Jill understood of the islands of Loch Lomond, they would be a faster search than those of the firth given their distance from shore and the limited buildings that might house a painting. Jill could see spending less than ten minutes on some islands.

Murray and Campbell returned to the room indicating they'd

made the boat and car plans and they should join them in heading down to the car park. Minutes later with Murray at the wheel and Jill in the front passenger seat they were negotiating mid-morning Edinburgh traffic.

CHAPTER 37

Not wanting to distract her driver, Jill kept the small talk to a minimum. They were out of the normal heavy traffic of the city and heading toward Glasgow and then on to Loch Lomond. Jill had checked, and it would be about an hour and a half to the southern part of the Loch. Fortunately, all the islands were in the southern part of the Loch. Jill hoped they had a speedboat at the Loch. With the Firth, she didn't know enough about speedboats versus cars to know which was faster to some of the islands on her list, but she guessed it was a car. When they arrived at the Duck Bay Marina, they had a local officer from West Dunbartonshire that was already at the motor of what looked to be a powerful patrol boat.

Once Campbell helped them push off from the dock, the three officers stood near the wheel chatting. Nathan and Jill had their cameras out ready to capture something new, while Michael and Nicole viewed the upcoming island with anticipation. The southernmost island was the biggest with the most structures on it. Fortunately, it was closed for the season which allowed them unfettered access to all of the buildings. The painting was about two feet by three feet, so a quick look in all rooms was all they needed to move on to the next island.

Jill watched Nicole's enthusiasm dropping as each island in the Loch disappointed them with the lack of a painting. Jill hoped to find the painting for Nick's legacy but was content to enjoy the Scottish countryside and this beautiful lake.

"Someday when you're not chasing a ten million dollar work of art, I would enjoy staying in one of those cabins on the first island we visited or better still the island with the private home on the last island," Nathan said. "I love the peace here."

"We could also stay on the island with the old distillery. Perhaps you could make some moonshine while we're there," Jill replied leaning against him with the wind buffeting her.

"I think I would likely poison the two of us trying that and our bodies would be rotted by the time someone visited our scene of death. I'll pass."

Jill laughed, "Imagine that you would think of a way of killing us before I would! You have a point about the old distillery. I suppose there might be rust and lead in our moonshine."

"At the very least, along with spiders, and mice vermin."

"Okay, you've killed it for me. Forget that I mentioned that unromantic idea of spending time there killing ourselves," Jill said with a shudder.

Soon they were ashore reloaded in the van and on their way back to Glasgow, Edinburgh and then on to a boat at the Firth. Nathan asked that they stop at a grocery store on their way through Glasgow so he could buy lunch for the group. Shortly they were back on the road munching on sandwiches. Murray had them arriving at the dock closest to Cramond Island in the early afternoon. She explained that they would return to the docks at Leith as the tide made it tricky for boats in this area.

The tide was out, so they walked across the causeway to the island. Jill noted the numerous tags of graffiti artists and the general dilapidated air of the building on the island and knew no painting could survive there. She said so to the group, but they dutifully searched the structures. They met the patrol boat manned by a new officer and made their way across the firth to the next island of her list.

Jill had high hopes for it as there was an old monastery located on it. Wouldn't that be a great place to hide an old painting? Furthermore, there was a purported thirteen-century wall painting in the Abbey which suggested that a painting would survive. She kept her thought to herself not wanting to dash Nicole's optimism if they came up empty-handed again. There was a WWII tunnel also on the island, but after looking at all of her prime suspected locations, Jill was now the one that was melancholy over not finding the painting.

Oh well, at least they were getting such stunning if not rapidly taken photographs of some beautiful islands.

They moved on to the next to the last island on her list. It had a lighthouse that was automated, but it was really quite sad from the decaying military fortifications of WWII and earlier. Before she set foot on the island, she thought the only likely place for the art to survive was in the lighthouse, but once she approached the yellow three or four-story structure and saw the impact of graffiti artists she knew the painting wasn't there.

It left one more island to explore and then the painting would fall into the cold case file in Edinburgh; a sad ending to what started as a highly anticipated journey. They boarded the boat and noted that depending on their trip to the final island; they would make it back to Edinburgh by sunset. Again she silently thanked the weather gods for a great day by Scottish standards.

Maybe she was feeling the fancifulness of Nicole, but as they approached this last island, she felt it calling out to her on the painting. It had a critical lighthouse, manned until the late 1980s. Could the painting have been left behind in the lighthouse or one of the houses occupied by birdwatchers on the island? Would no one have noticed its value? And how had it arrived on the island to start with? Did someone just dump it in one of the buildings hoping to forget that it had been stolen from someone running from the Nazis? Jill was not an art expert and couldn't answer these questions.

The island had served the military during WWII with men posted to look for German submarines approaching the Scottish coast, but that isn't how such a painting would have arrived.

As they approached the harbor, they noticed another boat already tied up there. She supposed it was for the bird experts; to bring supplies out to the islands. She looked around at everyone and said, "Well this is the end of the road for me. Either the painting will be here, or better minds than mine will have to find this missing Canaletto painting." Jill tossed off her life vest onto the boat and departed with everyone else. They walked up the road towards the original lighthouse powered by coal and oil with Michael and Nicole in the front and Nathan and Jill in the rear. There was also a little cluster of houses; it was very quiet so Jill assumed that the birds were active at dusk and thus the bird-watchers were out and about watching the birds.

She looked over at DIs Campbell and Murray and said, "Is this where you went to camp?"

It was an excellent question to ask as none of the islands had triggered that reaction yet. Maybe Jill had picked the wrong islands of Loch Lomond? When she looked over at the two detective inspectors though, they were frozen in place. Jill followed their gaze and saw what she initially missed.

CHAPTER 38

Her Italian man was standing in the doorway of the farthest row house, gun in hand.

She knew the Scottish DIs carried no guns, though they might be armed with Tasers. She hadn't thought to ask earlier given she'd expected no trouble.

Campbell called out to the man, "DI Campbell, Police Scotland, drop your gun."

The man made no move to follow orders.

"He speaks Italian," Jill said in a softer voice. Jill could see Campbell put the pieces together to determine who this man was holding a gun on them that Jill knew.

Campbell asked Michael to translate his command for him and he did, but the Italian man didn't move or otherwise indicate he was going to follow the command.

Jill said to Michael, "Ask him if he found the treasure." She listened as Michael translated the question and watched as the armed man reached for something at his knees to show them what appeared to be a painting.

Michael followed up with a question of his own and the man

replied. Michael explained to the group that when he returned home, he found a small notebook belonging to his friend Girard in his luggage and he indicated the location of the painting on this island.

Jill thought thankfully Italy is far from this corner of Scotland so it took the man so long to get back that they could intercept him. She looked sideways at Nathan and found he'd disappeared. She took another quick look and then decided he must be planning something. Oh dear!

DI Campbell told Michael to tell the man he was under arrest for threatening a police officer, owning a gun, and stealing property from the government of Scotland. Michael repeated the order, and a few sentences were exchanged.

Michael turned back to Campbell and said, "He doesn't care what you say. He has a gun and if you don't move out of his way, he'll shoot one or all of us. He's planning on leaving on his boat with the painting."

Jill wondered if there were birdwatchers inside the building either dead or restrained? She also worried about where Nathan had gone.

The Italian man steadied his grip on the gun, which in Jill's eyes looked like a semi-automatic weapon. If he wanted, he could mow them all down where they stood. Jill backed away from the path trying to give him space as she saw the others doing out of the corner of her eye.

Campbell caught her eye and seemed to note that Nathan was missing. The Italian man said something in Italian which Michael translated as, "He says stay back, or he'll be forced to shoot us."

The gunman slowly moved forward watching all of them; gun clasped in one hand, the painting in the other. He was inching forward from a slate grey house to a whitewashed house. Jill wondered at the different architecture and then refocused on the man with a gun. She caught sight of Nathan on the roof of the white building; she was worried that the gunmen would detect him and shoot, so she turned toward the harbor and pointed, saying, "Look is that another boat coming?"

Everyone looked including the gunman, and since he didn't understand English, Jill felt reasonably secure saying in a low voice to Campbell nearest to her, "I'm just trying to distract everyone from Nathan."

The gunman continued to walk down the path toward the dock, while Nathan edged over the roof. Thank goodness it was an ancient stone house designed to withstand the vigorous weather of an island in the North Sea.

Nathan grabbed a stone or ceramic drain pipe and swung off the roof and into the man's back plunging him forward. In seconds Murray and Campbell were on the man separating him from his gun. Nicole and Michael made a dive for the painting wanting to see it safe. Jill had her eyes on Nathan the whole time hoping that he would remain unharmed from his daring maneuver.

She needn't have worried. He ended up with filthy hands and a cut on one finger. She ran over to him, hugging him for dear life. He just leaned down with a smile and said, "That was fun, now I've got a great story to tell friends."

"What? About the time you caused my heart to beat so fast that the Scottish Police had to get a defibrillator off their boat to shock it to a slower pace?"

"Come'on babe, admit it, you're jealous that I thought of circling behind the man and you didn't. That was a modified stomp kick that would have made my Sensei proud," Nathan said wearing one of his rare wildly happy smiles.

She had to mask a grin of her own, and she turned and looked at the others. Seeing the Italian man secured, she looked over to the painting to find Michael with a magnifying glass examining the painting. From this distance, it looked unharmed.

Campbell was holding the man down with handcuffs on him. Murray was on the phone, and she saw the officer from the boat running up the path toward their aid. When the officer arrived, Campbell directed him to search the man for additional weapons. During the search, they found his passport.

"So your Italian man's name is Giovanni Floris and he lives in Sardinia. I assume this is the man that used a stun gun on you and you decided not to contact police. Have you changed your mind?"

Jill thought about it and said, "I think you probably have enough charges on the man without my adding to them. I'd like to stay out of the Scottish justice system."

"Are you sure? What he did was serious. It was an armed assault," Murray added.

Campbell must have mentioned that story to Murray when Jill was out of hearing range.

"Yes. I'm sure. As much as I've enjoyed your company Detective Inspectors, I'll be leaving for the United States in the morning. I would like to leave with the case closed. I'll give you a statement today about the events on the island, and I'll be able to leave understanding the motive for Nick's murder. I would be interested in hearing what Mr. Floris says once you have an official translator and question him. I think that valuable painting was the cause of Nick's death," Jill said pointing to the painting.

Murray said to Campbell, "We have reinforcements and crime scene technicians on the way. Also, a contact from the Museum is joining them to make sure we move the painting with appropriate care. I imagine that letting the sea breeze whip it on the way back to shore is a terrible way to take care of a ten million pound painting."

Jill checked the time and said, "Is there any way we civilians can be transported back to Edinburgh once those reinforcements arrive?"

"Yes we'll make those arrangements after we take all of your contact information down. You will all need to make a statement, but we'll have other detectives assist with that."

Michael asked, "Is there anything you would like me to say to Mr. Floris?"

Campbell thought for a moment then shook his head, "He needs to be read his rights by an official translator. I've shown him my shield, so he knows who we are. Even if you can't read English, most police badges look alike."

Jill thought of something, "Ask him if there are any hostages inside the house?"

Murray answered for him, "We checked with the ferry company and the Bird Society and knew before we arrived that there were no permanent residents here this week. I assume the boat down at the dock belongs to him, but we'll do a search of all the buildings on this island just to be sure, as there's nothing stopping anyone from visiting the island by private boat as you can see. It's going to be a long night here, and I'm sure there 'll be a press conference tonight as well in downtown Edinburgh as this is a major piece of stolen art."

Campbell added cynically, "Just got to prove to the public that we coppers are giving them their tax dollars."

Jill looked up as she saw a helicopter approaching. Murray and Campbell also squinted at it and said, "Wow the brass is pulling out all the resources for this case - that's our only police helicopter in all of Scotland. Maybe they can give you a quick ride back to the mainland."

They watched the helicopter land at a site near the lighthouse on the top of the hill. A party of men and a woman descended the path down the hill toward them, and she saw Murray and Campbell snap to attention.

"Bloody hell, it's the Chief and his minions," muttered Murray to Campbell.

Campbell was moving his attention between the approaching

party and Mr. Floris, who was lying compliant on the ground, restrained with the officer guarding him.

The Chief had obviously been briefed about the painting as Jill noted that DCS Craig was at the back of the party. She bet he'd had a great job of explaining who the civilians were on the case. She thought Nathan was correct; they would have an exciting story to tell their friends.

His party approached, and introductions were made. The Chief said, "This is one of the more unusual cases during my time as Chief. We're holding a press conference early in the morning, and I thought it was best to get my ducks in order by visiting the crime scene and meeting the people involved. DCS Craig has briefed me on the way over, but DI Murray and Campbell, I would like to hear your report about the events today. After that, I would like to hear from the civilians. Perhaps there is somewhere we can take our suspect to hold him in more comfortable surroundings while we await the arrival of more officers."

The two DIs moved off a few feet away for a discussion with their Chief. DCS Craig assisted the officer from the boat with hefting Mr. Floris to his feet and moving him down the path to a rock to sit on while under guard. Jill noticed that he had a bloody nose and upper lip which spoke to the speed at which he descended to the ground after Nathan's stomp kick to his shoulders.

Nicole and Michael were holding the painting with white gloves. She hadn't seen the gloves before now, but she supposed those were tools of the trade when dealing with precious art. Nathan had poured water on the cut on his hand and Jill produced a band-aid from her purse to cover up the still bleeding cut.

"You'll live. I don't think there is any danger of you bleeding to death, although you should get a tetanus shot as there might have been some Clostridium on that roof from dust or bird poop," Jill speculated eyeing the roof.

"Got my tetanus about three years ago. How long is it good for? I thought a decade."

"Yeah, that's generally true. I'd feel better if we could rinse the cut with something stronger than water. Let me see if there's a first aid kit on the helicopter or boat; then I could clean it up properly," so saying she walked down to where Mr. Floris was resting and asked directions to the kit in the boat. By the time she located and returned with the kit, the Chief was done with listening to his detectives and was moving towards her.

"I was unaware that any civilians sustained any injuries during this incident."

"She's a forensic pathologist just wanting to make sure I don't end up dead on her table," quipped Nathan. "I cut my hand on the roof as I swung down to kick Mr. Floris. It's a minor injury already treated. With any luck, I'll have a scar to remind me of this episode."

The Chief smiled at Nathan's remarks and said, "If you're not comfortable having a pathologist treat your wound, our pilot is a medic."

"I think your Mr. Floris might need his care more than I," Nathan replied as they looked at the bloodied face.

"Ah yes," said the Chief as he asked one of his party to get some care for Mr. Floris.

He returned to Nathan and Jill and said, "I have a new respect for my detectives for listening to your story this morning and joining you in the hunt for the painting. I would not have put our resources into play. My detectives filled me in on some of your other cases, so I guess I understand why they threw caution to the wind to assist you and I'm grateful they did. I think I have a good summary of what happened here, but I'd like to hear about the death of your friend in Wales and how that fits with this case. I understand that is what started the ball rolling on this case."

"My friends and I were here for a long-planned vacation in the

United Kingdom. We expected to meet our friend Nick Brouwer from the Netherlands here."

"My condolences on his death. I understand that he has no family and you and a friend in Germany are taking care of his arrangements? Is he connected to your private detective company?"

Jill provided an explanation of the case where she met Nick and Henrik and how they helped her since.

"So I got an odd explanation about a stay-behind army from one of my detectives. Can you explain that to me?"

"Actually, if you can crack your suspect, I would guess that he knows the most. We've never had the opportunity to verify our theory about all of these men - Nick, Girard, and Giovanni belonging to a secret army, but it makes some sense," Jill replied providing an overview of stay-behind armies from WWII.

"What would be their motive for searching for or stealing a painting dating back to the looting of the Nazi's from what I understand?"

"I wondered that myself. The Allies set up a group of army staff and art experts at the end of the war to recover art and return it to their rightful owners. There are still many famous pieces missing from that war that are thought to be in private collections or had been destroyed during the act of fighting the war. I can't begin to guess how this Canaletto painting ended up on this island - was it a previous tenant? Did someone hide it here in plain sight? They took a chance that none of the birdwatchers staying here over the years thought to remove or destroy it. I'll leave the provenance of that painting to the experts. I understand that it will need to be examined for the age of the pigment and canvas. It'll make a nice visual at a press conference, but I don't know if it's real; sure seems that way."

He spoke a little more with them and moved on to the art experts for a short conversation. Jill had a feeling he was collecting sound bites to use in his upcoming press conference.

He took a picture of the painting. In the end, he offered them a ride back to Edinburgh just as a large boat was arriving with the experts that the detectives mentioned earlier. Nicole and Michael wanted to stay to discuss the painting with the promised art experts.

CHAPTER 39

Soon they were whizzing back toward Edinburgh. They were informed that they'd be dropped off at the Edinburgh Racecourse at which an officer was waiting to take them back to their hotel about five miles away. Once they landed, Jill noted it was a horse race course not a car racetrack and a short time later they returned to their hotel. A detective would stop by the hotel to record their testimony later, as they had an early flight in the morning.

"Where do you want to go to eat?" Jill asked as they returned to their hotel room after a full day of adventure.

They knocked around some cuisine ideas while checking in with Campbell as to how soon a detective could be sent to their location to record their statements. The detective suggested they go to dinner and he would have a detective reach them at their hotel later. They settled on a lively pub. They both were still on an emotional high over the day's activities. Jill was hungry for meat and potatoes while Nathan wanted one last whiskey tasting session. Before they left the hotel, she'd dropped an email to Marie, Angela, and Jo about the day's discovery adding that they could likely find the story on the internet the next day.

They had finished their meals and were both leaning back relaxed in each other's company, and the world at large. Though the pub was noisy, it had a calming effect on them or at least it did until a special news bulletin came on the air saying that there would be a special police press conference the next morning at six. The newscaster went on to read that inside sources said the press conference would be related to an old crime from WWII.

"That's a brilliant approach to putting the most positive spin on today's events," Nathan mused.

"Yeah and by delaying it until tomorrow morning, I bet they might have some analysis of the painting to know if it's real. The announcement also gives news organizations normally not present in Edinburgh, a chance to get here by tomorrow morning. I think this Chief is brilliant as far as how he's telling the world about this recovery."

The news went back to the regular programming, and they listened a while to the pub patrons to see what if anything, they made of the news. It seemed that about half of them moved to other subjects, while others speculated that the police had found an old grave of someone that had been murdered.

As they returned to the hotel, they saw a Police Scotland car in front and thought their detective must have arrived. They entered and saw a man in a dark suit and Jill called out, "Detective?"

He turned around from the desk assistant and smiled at them, "Dr. Quint?"

She nodded, and he said, "I took a chance that you'd be done with dinner and it seems I misjudged the time by about ten minutes."

"Actually it's your Chief's fault. We caught the announcement of the press conference tomorrow morning and stayed to hear what people were saying in speculation in the pub."

The detective had frowned when Jill said it was his Chief's fault, but then his glorious smile returned as he said, "That was cheeky of him. I need to get your statements. Is there a room we can use here in the hotel?"

"If you don't mind our messy hotel room, we could do it there. We have a tiny sitting area."

"Okay."

Jill and Nathan took their turns reciting their stories while the other wore noise-canceling headphones that the detective had brought for the statements. They didn't want their stories to appear to have been corroborated and the headphones did the trick.

The interview took an hour mostly getting Jill's details about the bigger components of the case and how her research took them to the final island that day. He packed up his equipment to leave adding, "Detectives Murray and Campbell are driving you to the airport in the morning and will escort you through security. They'll be here at eight sharp to see that you make your flight."

"That's very kind of them," Nathan said.

"Probably just want to make sure I leave their territory," Jill joked. "Please pass on our thanks to the detectives and we'll be ready."

They closed the door on the detective, finished packing their suitcases and fell into bed, exhausted after such an action-packed day.

Jill was up with the birds and tuned the television in to watch the Chief's press conference. As she thought, they had done some verification of the painting. They had an age range on it dating to Canaletto's time, but it required more study by art experts. She appreciated that he didn't state her name for the record, but referred to her as a private detective from California. He mentioned two agents from Brisdale's and that the painting was stolen from an Amsterdam art merchant who had fled the coming Nazi invasion. The Chief had no explanation of how it ended up on the island, just that it had been there at least thirty years, untouched by birdwatchers. She saw Campbell, Murray, and

Craig standing behind the Chief. He had Campbell step up to the podium to relay their treasure hunt the previous day. By the end of the press conference, there was no mention of Mr. Floris or a secret army. Jill couldn't find fault with anything said during the press conference, so she turned back to getting ready for a long flight home.

Jill went down to the hotel's café for a carafe of coffee needed to wake Nathan up and breakfast. She returned to the room, waking him up and once assured that he would stay awake, she went back to her own breakfast and email. She rather liked that Nathan didn't talk in the morning as he was slow to awaken. She could get a nice start to the day while leaving him to his own speed of waking up. She left out the few things he needed to wear, shower, or shave with and had their bags ready to go. She was glad of their escort as she felt assured the airport security process would be fast and she wanted to hear more about what they discovered that wasn't said during the press conference.

They had their bags at the curb and were enjoying a Scottish mist when the van of yesterday pulled to the curb. Campbell got out to help load their bags in the back saying, "I know you Americans carry a lot of luggage and we were afraid it wouldn't fit in a squad car, so I asked for the prisoner wagon, but it was in use, so we settled for yesterday's car."

"Ha ha," Jill said. "I'm glad I brought just one case so you can't complain about my luggage. Saw you at the press conference; you did well."

"Thanks, the Chief didn't want to talk about Mr. Floris or the stay-behind army at his press conference. It took us a while to think of a story flow that would leave out some of the details."

"How's the public receiving the news? I'm sure you've had some feedback by now."

"I think most people are pleased that we're restoring a possession to a family that likely lost everything in WWII including their lives. The other comments I've heard relate to the painting going unnoticed by the birders."

Murray added, "People have been making comments about bird people being blind to everything but birds. It is amusing that they missed a ten million pound painting in front of their binoculars."

"Was it in the house on the wall? I wondered what Mr. Floris said under questioning as to the painting's location."

"He said it was in what looked to be a study in the house. The study was filled with reference guides on birds and a bird poster was covering up much of the painting. We asked him how Girard or Nick found the painting, but he didn't know, he simply followed the instructions in the notebook to find the painting."

"Did you find out when you visited the island as a kid in camp?"

"Yeah, it was driving me crazy. So when I returned to my house late last night, I pulled out some old photo albums and found a picture of this island in one of them. Our camp director must have taken us into the study to show us bird books or posters and we saw the painting then. I think it must have planted itself deep in my brain to find this odd Italian painting with bird books. I think at that age I might have thought the books were about the birds in the picture."

"That's good, at least one mystery has been solved," Jill said. "I still don't know how Nick found it. He never struck me as a bird fancier, but then again who knows where his travels took him in their secret stay-behind army."

After taking a breath, she peppered the DI's with more questions, "Did you learn anything else from Mr. Floris? What was he going to do with the painting? Has the family that the painting belongs to said anything? Were you able to get any details of the group he belonged to? Does he speak Guernésiais? Did he say there was anything else of interest in the notebook that pointed him to the island?"

"Whoa, that's a lot of questions. What's Guernésiais?" asked Murray.

"It's a rare language originating from the island of Guernsey. We found emails and text messages on Nick's phone in that language," Jill replied. "I figured it was the language of the secret group they belonged to. You might use that question to see if you can crack Mr. Solis. My limited experience with him, suggested he was not the sharpest tool in the shed, but a very willing follower."

"What's that expression?" asked Murray trying to puzzle the words.

"I'm sure you have a Scottish expression for it," Jill laughed. "It means that he didn't appear to me to be the smartest criminal."

"Failing means you're playing," Murray said.

"What?" Jill laughed.

"Even if you're lousy at something, at least you're in the game is how I would describe our Mr. Floris. I think he'll be our guest for a long time as I'm betting MI6 might want to ask him some questions. We'll keep him out of the public's eye until we decide what to do with him. In the end, he might just get deported home," Campbell said. "As to what he was going to do with the painting, I don't think he knew; he hadn't thought much beyond finding it. We haven't finished questioning him so I'll add your question about the notebook. Maybe Italian authorities will give Girard LeRoux's notebook to us. As for the family that rightfully owns the painting, we haven't made a notification yet pending verification from our art experts that it's real and the people that it belongs to are the legitimate heirs. It's way beyond my pay grade."

They were pulling up to the airport and Jill could see another officer pulling up cones so they could park. After parking and introducing the officer that would escort their party through security, they continued into the terminal to their airline desk where they were swiftly helped with their luggage, tickets, and passports. From there they found a fast escort through security as well.

Campbell added, "I didn't feel that threatened by him and his gun yesterday as he never had his finger on the trigger. So we have a wide range of things we could charge him with, but the spooks and government might think it best to just send him home."

"You know I'd be happy to assist Police Scotland at any time if I can get this service at the airport," Jill said admiring the service.

"Jill, I think it's like you said last night, they just want to be sure we leave their territory," Nathan added.

Murray and Campbell smiled.

"I think we'll have less crime with your absence," Campbell said.

"Hey now, we do appreciate your help yesterday with Mr. Floris and the painting and all," Murray said.

"But you're telling me that Nathan got that cut on his hand for nothing as you were never really worried about Mr. Floris and his gun."

"Here's another Scottish expression, 'long may your chimney smoke'," Campbell said choosing valor over truth as he and Murray had come to a stop at their airplane gate.

"I believe you're wishing us a long life with that expression," Nathan said. "I think I heard that at one of the distilleries I visited as a toast."

They both nodded and held out their hands to shake in farewell, and then Nathan and Jill got in line for their final passport inspection and carry-on luggage search.

A few weeks later...

Henrik had arranged many aspects of the memorial service. Nick's body had been held at a mortuary until they could gather for a proper funeral. It was a small private affair of their immediate group and Nick's employees at a church in Stuttgart. The burial would be private and limited to the six of them on Henrik's property.

The five of them had flown in for the weekend, starting the memorial service with readings by a pastor and speeches by Jill and Angela, and one of his employees. After the service, there was a small reception in the church hall. No one had any idea of how strong Nick's religious values were, so they tried for a moderate ceremony. Without a will, Nick's company would have failed had Henrik not stepped in and provided capital and legal help to see that it continued as a tiny part of his corporation.

They were surprised by the attendance of the family that had contacted Nick years before to find their father's Canaletto painting. They learned more details about Nick through that conversation. Nick had helped another family find a lost painting stolen by the Nazis and this family contacted Nick to help. They provided him a picture of the painting and he promised to search for it.

A year went by and Nick let them know he had no leads yet. About nine months later, he contacted them and said he had a lead that the painting had been sighted in the U.K. which excited them that they might have the painting after more than seventy years.

"What kind of a lead?" Angela asked.

"He came across the word Canaletto in reference to an estate," the son said.

"Apparently the last of an ancient family had died with no heirs and so the property reverted to the government of the United Kingdom. There was a list of the properties and valuables conferred upon the government including mention of the painting. From there Nick had to visit all of the properties of this British Lord to physically search for the painting. He had been visiting the properties over several months and had to covertly examine the properties because it wasn't as if the new owners wanted him on their land be it the government or a new private owner. He almost gave up when he chanced upon it on an island. The Lord had an island that became a bird conservancy and it was the last place he'd thought he would find it."

"Why didn't he immediately alert the authorities so he could remove the painting?" Jo asked.

"He found he was being followed by someone he knew, but was highly suspicious of and he didn't want to get our hopes up so he had some friends that could verify the provenance of the painting. This man knew he'd been out on the island but hadn't known what he was looking for. He didn't want to report the acquaintance and hoped they would work out the issues. Then next we heard, Nick had been murdered."

"This acquaintance is also dead and from what we knew of

him, Nick was right in thinking the guy would steal the painting for himself," Jill said.

"We didn't know the name of the Lord or where the island was in the United Kingdom and as you know there are about one hundred islands, so we planned to start over with a new detective and were just interviewing people when we saw the news about the painting. How did you and your team find it?"

"I think the painting was calling for itself to be returned to its rightful owner. It was pure luck that when I showed the detectives that they had remembered seeing it in their childhoods at a camp. Once I heard that I was able to limit the prospective islands down to seven."

"Would you have an interest in searching on behalf of other families that are still searching for their lost art or jewelry?"

"Probably not," Jill replied. "I'm a doctor by training and so I usually investigate someone's murder, not their stolen possessions. Besides, I and my team have a lack of understanding about Europe's cities and history. At one point in this investigation, we were looking at concentration camps in Northern Europe and I was totally unaware of what happened to the Jewish population in Estonia during WWII. That lack of knowledge would probably inhibit my effectiveness as an investigator. Other families that are still searching would be better served to pick someone with that intuitive knowledge. What will you do with the painting once it's confirmed to belong to your family?"

"We wanted the painting back for our grandfather's sake, but now that we have it we don't want to keep it as a reminder of his terrible death. We'll likely send it to auction and use the proceeds to support programs that teach diversity and tolerance. We think he would have been pleased by that function of the painting's proceeds."

Jill nodded at that idea understanding the family's thoughts on the painting. The service came to an end and it was time that they depart with Nick's remains to Henrik's home through the

German countryside which was now in deep fall with the leaves an array of brilliant colors. Jill found poetry in brilliant colors as matching the flames of Nick's soul before being extinguished with the arrival of winter.

Henrik consulted with them on his thoughts of where to bury their good friend Nick. His late wife held a plot along a walking path from his house. It didn't make sense to bury Nick there as he wasn't family. Instead, they buried him on an obstacle course that Henrik had created for the security of his house and company. It was occasionally used by German and Belgian special forces for training. They thought Nick would want to be in the thick of it, even in death. So he had a grave near where Henrik had laid a trap of green goo that would cover any intruder trying to get in. Nick had always laughed hugely every time he watched the green goo catch someone by surprise in a training exercise. Now he could laugh for eternity.

The End

ABOUT THE AUTHOR

I reside in Northern California with my rescue dog and cat. I love to travel, play sports, read, and drink wine and beer. I enjoy the diversity of the world and I'm always watching people and events for story ideas.

If you would like to sign up for my monthly blog and announcement of new books, please follow this link: https://www.AlecPecheBooks.com

While you're waiting for the next story, if you would be so kind as to leave a review for this book, that would be great. I appreciate all the feedback and support. Reviews buoy my spirits and stoke the fires of creativity.

Readers that sign up for website receive a free prequel novelette for the Jill Quint Series.

Author Profile on Goodreads

Author Profile on BookBub

How Did She Get There? (2022)